IN THE

FLESH

CLIVE BARKER

POSEIDON PRESS
New York

COPYRIGHT © 1986 BY CLIVE BARKER
ALL RIGHTS RESERVED
INCLUDING THE RIGHT OF REPRODUCTION
IN WHOLE OR IN PART IN ANY FORM
PUBLISHED BY POSEIDON PRESS
A DIVISION OF SIMON & SCHUSTER, INC.
SIMON & SCHUSTER BUILDING
ROCKEFELLER CENTER
1230 AVENUE OF THE AMERICAS
NEW YORK, NEW YORK 10020
ORIGINALLY PUBLISHED IN GREAT BRITAIN BY SPHERE BOOKS LTD.
UNDER THE TITLE *BOOKS OF BLOOD, VOLUME V.*
POSEIDON PRESS IS A REGISTERED TRADEMARK OF
SIMON & SCHUSTER, INC.
DESIGNED BY IRVING PERKINS ASSOCIATES
MANUFACTURED IN THE UNITED STATES OF AMERICA
1 3 5 7 9 10 8 6 4 2
LIBRARY OF CONGRESS CATALOGING-IN-PUBLICATION DATA
PARKER, CLIVE, DATE–
IN THE FLESH.

CONTENTS: IN THE FLESH—THE FORBIDDEN—THE
MADONNA—BABEL'S CHILDREN.
1. HORROR TALES, AMERICAN.   I. TITLE.
PR6052.A6475I48   1987   823'.914   86-20450
ISBN: 0-671-62687-6

BY CLIVE BARKER:

**THE INHUMAN CONDITION
IN THE FLESH**

TO
JULIE

CONTENTS

IN THE
FLESH

WHEN CLEVELAND SMITH RETURNED TO HIS CELL AFTER the interview with the Landing Officer, his new bunk-mate was already in residence, staring at the dust-infested sunlight through the reinforced glass window. It was a short display; for less than half an hour each afternoon (clouds permitting) the sun found its way between the wall and the administration building and edged its way along the side of B Wing, not to appear again until the following day.

"You're Tait?" Cleve said.

The prisoner looked away from the sun. Mayflower had said the new boy was twenty-two, but Tait looked five years younger. He had the face of a lost dog. An ugly dog, at that—a dog left by its owners to play in traffic. Eyes too wide, mouth too soft, arms too slender: a born victim. Cleve was irritated to have been encumbered with the boy. Tait was dead weight, and Cleve had no energies to expend on the boy's protection, despite Mayflower's pep talk about extending a welcoming hand.

"Yes," the dog replied. "William."

"People call you William?"

"No," the boy said. "They call me Billy."

"Billy." Cleve nodded, and stepped into the cell. The regime at Pentonville was relatively enlightened; cells were left open for two hours in the mornings, and often two in the afternoon, allowing the cons some freedom of movement. The arrangement had its disadvantages, however, which was where Mayflower's talk came in.

"I've been told to give you some advice."

"Oh?" the boy replied.

"You've not done time before?"

"No."

11

"Not even Borstal?"

Tait's eyes flickered. "A little."

"So you know what the score is. You know you're easy meat."

"Sure."

"Seems I've been volunteered," Cleve said without appetite, "to keep you from getting mauled."

Tait stared at Cleve with eyes the blue of which was milky, as though the sun were still in them. "Don't put yourself out," the boy said. "You don't owe me anything."

"Damn right I don't. But it seems I got a social responsibility," Cleve said sourly. "And you're it."

•

Cleve was two months into his sentence for handling marijuana, his third visit to Pentonville. At thirty years of age he was far from obsolete. His body was solid, his face lean and refined; in his court suit he could have passed for a lawyer at ten yards. A little closer, and the viewer might catch the scar on his neck, the result of an attack by a penniless addict, and a certain wariness in his gait, as if with every step forward he was keeping the option of a speedy retreat.

You're still a young man, the last judge had told him; you still have time to change your spots. He hadn't disagreed out loud, but Cleve knew in his heart he was a leopard born and bred. Crime was easy, work was not. Until somebody proved otherwise he would do what he did best, and take the consequences if caught. Doing time wasn't so unpalatable if you had the right attitude toward it. The food was edible, the company select; as long as he had something to keep his mind occupied he was content enough. At present he was reading about sin. Now *there* was a subject. In his time he'd heard so many explanations of how it had come into the world, from probation officers and lawyers and priests. Theories sociological, theological, ideological. Some were worthy of a few minutes' consideration. Most were so absurd (sin from the womb, sin from the state) he laughed in their apologists' faces. None held water for long.

It was a good bone to chew over, though. He needed a problem to occupy the days. And nights; he slept badly in prison. It wasn't *his* guilt that kept him awake but that of others. He was, after all, just a hash pusher, supplying wherever there was a demand: a minor cog in the consumerist machine, he had nothing to feel guilty about. But there were others here, *many* others, it seemed, whose dreams were not so benevolent, nor nights so peaceful. They would cry, they would complain, they would curse judges local and celestial. Their din would have kept the dead awake.

"Is it always like this?" Billy asked Cleve after a week or so. A new inmate was making a ruckus down the landing: one moment tears, the next obscenities.

"Yes. Most of the time," said Cleve. "Some of them need to yell a bit. It keeps their minds from curdling."

"Not you," observed the unmusical voice from the bunk below, "you just read your books and keep out of harm's way. I've watched you. It doesn't bother you, does it?"

"I can live with it," Cleve replied. "I got no wife to come here every week and remind me what I'm missing."

"You been in before?"

"Twice."

The boy hesitated an instant before saying, "I suppose you know your way around the place, do you?"

"Well, I'm not writing a guidebook, but I got the general layout by now." It seemed an odd comment for the boy to make. "Why?"

"I just wondered," said Billy.

"You got a question?"

Tait didn't answer for several seconds, then said: "I heard they used to . . . used to *hang* people here."

Whatever Cleve had been expecting the boy to come out

with, that wasn't it. But then he had decided several days back that Billy Tait was a strange one. Sly, sidelong glances from those milky-blue eyes; a way he had of staring at the wall or at the window like a detective at a murder scene, desperate for clues.

Cleve said, "There used to be a hanging shed, I think."

Again silence, and then another inquiry, dropped as lightly as the boy could contrive. "Is it still standing?"

"The shed? I don't know. They don't hang people anymore, Billy, or hadn't you heard?" There was no reply from below. "What's it to you, anyhow?"

"Just curious."

•

Billy was right; curious he was. So odd, with his vacant stares and his solitary manner, that most of the men kept clear of him. Only Lowell took any interest in him, and his motives for that were unequivocal.

"You want to lend me your lady for the afternoon?" he asked Cleve while they waited in line for breakfast. Tait, who stood within earshot, said nothing; neither did Cleve.

"You hear me? I asked you a question."

"I heard. You leave him alone."

"Share and share alike," Lowell said. "I can do you some favors. We can work something out."

"He's not available."

"Well, why don't I ask *him*?" Lowell said, grinning through his beard. "What do you say, baby?"

Tait looked around at Lowell.

"I say no thank you."

"No *thank you*," Lowell said, and gave Cleve a second smile, this quite without humor. "You've got him well trained. Does he sit up and beg, too?"

"Take a walk, Lowell," Cleve replied. "He's not available and that's all there is to it."

"You can't keep your eyes on him every minute of the day," Lowell pointed out. "Sooner or later he's going to have to stand on his own two feet. Unless he's better kneeling."

The innuendo won a guffaw from Lowell's cell-mate, Nayler. Neither were men Cleve would have willingly faced in a free-for-all, but his skills as a bluffer were honed razor-sharp, and he used them now.

"You don't want to trouble yourself," he told Lowell. "You can only cover so many scars with a beard."

Lowell looked at Cleve, all humor fled. He clearly couldn't distinguish the truth from bluff, and equally clearly wasn't willing to put his neck on the line.

"Just don't look the other way," he said, and said no more.

•

The encounter at breakfast wasn't mentioned until that night when the lights had been extinguished. It was Billy who brought it up.

"You shouldn't have done that," he said. "Lowell's a bad bastard. I've heard the talk."

"You want to get raped then, do you?"

"No," he said quickly, "Christ no. I got to be fit."

"You'll be fit for nothing if Lowell gets his hands on you."

Billy slipped out from his bunk and stood in the middle of the cell, barely visible in the gloom. "I suppose you want something in return," he said.

Cleve turned on his pillow and looked at the uncertain silhouette standing a yard from him. "What have you got that I'd want, Billy Boy?" he said.

"What Lowell wanted."

"Is that what you think that bluster was all about? Me staking a claim?"

"Yeah."

"Like you said: no thank you." Cleve rolled over again to face the wall.

"I didn't mean—"

"I don't care what you meant. I just don't want to hear about it, all right? You stay out of Lowell's way, and don't give me shit."

"Hey," Billy murmured, "don't get like that, please. *Please*. You're the only one friend I've got."

"I'm nobody's friend," Cleve said to the wall. "I just don't want any inconvenience. Understand me?"

"No inconvenience," the boy repeated, dull-tongued.

"Right. Now . . . I need my beauty sleep."

Tait said no more but returned to the bottom bunk and lay down, the springs creaking as he did so. Cleve lay in silence, turning the exchange over in his head. He had no wish to lay hands on the boy, but perhaps he had made his point too harshly. Well, it was done.

From below he could hear Billy murmuring to himself, almost inaudibly. He strained to eavesdrop on what the boy was saying. It took several seconds of ear-pricking attention before Cleve realized that Billy Boy was saying his prayers.

•

Cleve dreamed that night. What of, he couldn't remember in the morning, though as he showered and shaved tantalizing grains of the dream sifted through his head. Scarcely ten minutes went by that morning without something—salt overturned on the breakfast table, the sound of shouts in the exercise yard—promising to break his dream, but the revelation did not come. It left him uncharacteristically edgy and short-tempered. When Wesley, a small-time forger whom he knew from his previous vacation here, approached him in the library and started to talk as though they were bosom pals, Cleve told the runt to shut up. But Wesley insisted on speaking.

"You got trouble."

"Oh. How so?"

"That boy of yours. Billy."

"What about him?"

"He's asking questions. He's getting pushy. People don't like it. They're saying you should take him in hand."

"I'm not his keeper."

Wesley pulled a face. "I'm telling you, as a friend."

"Spare me."

"Don't be stupid, Cleveland. You're making enemies."

"Oh?" said Cleve. "Name one."

"Lowell," Wesley said, quick as a flash. "Nayler for another. All kinds of people. They don't like the way Tait is."

"And how is he?" Cleve snapped back.

Wesley made a small grunt of protest. "I'm just trying to tell you," he said. "He's sly. Like a fucking rat. There'll be trouble."

"Spare me the prophecies."

•

The law of averages demands the worst prophet be right some of the time: this was Wesley's moment, it seemed. The day after, coming back from the workshop, where he'd exercised his intellect putting wheels on plastic cars, Cleve found Mayflower waiting for him on the landing.

"I asked you to look after William Tait, Smith," the officer said. "Don't you give a damn?"

"What's happened?"

"No, I suppose you don't."

"I asked what happened. Sir."

"Nothing much. Not this time. He's been roughed up, that's all. Seems Lowell has a hankering after him. Am I right?" Mayflower peered at Cleve, and when he got no response went on: "I made an error with you, Smith. I thought there was something worth appealing to under the hard man. My mistake."

Billy was lying on the bunk, his face bruised, his eyes closed. He didn't open them when Cleve came in.

"You O.K.?"

"Sure," the boy said softly.

"No bones broken?"

"I'll survive."

"You've got to understand—"

"*Listen.*" Billy opened his eyes. The pupils had darkened somehow, or that was the trick the light performed with them. "I'm alive, O.K.? I'm not an idiot, you know. I knew what I was letting myself in for, coming here." He spoke as if he'd had a choice in the matter. "I can take Lowell," he went on, "so don't fret." He paused, then said, "You were right."

"About what?"

"About not having friends. I'm on my own, you're on your own. Right? I'm just a slow learner, but I'm getting the hang of it." He smiled to himself.

"You've been asking questions," Cleve said.

"Oh, yeah?" Billy replied off-handedly. "Who says?"

"If you've got questions, ask me. People don't like snoopers. They get suspicious. And then they turn their backs when Lowell and his like get heavy."

Naming the man brought a painful frown to Billy's face. He touched his bruised cheek. "He's dead," the boy murmured, almost to himself.

"Some chance," Cleve commented.

The look that Tait returned could have sliced steel. "I mean it," he said, without a trace of doubt in his voice. "Lowell won't get out alive."

Cleve didn't comment; the boy needed this show of bravado, laughable as it was.

"What do you want to know that you go snooping around?"

"Nothing much," Billy replied. He was no longer looking at Cleve but staring at the bunk above. Quietly, he said, "I just wanted to know where the graves were, that was all."

"The graves?"

"Where they buried the men they'd hanged. Somebody told

me there's a rose bush where Crippen's buried. You ever hear that?"

Cleve shook his head. Only now did he remember the boy asking about the hanging shed, and now the graves. Billy looked up at him. The bruise was ripening by the minute.

"You know where they are, Cleve?" he asked. Again, that feigned nonchalance.

"I could find out, if you do me the courtesy of telling me why you want to know."

Billy looked out from the shelter of the bunk. The afternoon sun was describing its short arc on the painted brick of the cell wall. It was weak today. The boy slid his legs off the bunk and sat on the edge of the mattress, staring at the light as he had on that first day.

"My grandfather—that is, my mother's father—was hanged here," he said, his voice raw. "In 1937. Edgar Tait. Edgar Saint Clair Tait."

"I thought you said your *mother's* father?"

"I took his name. I didn't want my father's name. I never belonged to him."

"Nobody belongs to anybody," Cleve replied. "You're your own man."

"But that's not true," Billy said with a tiny shrug, still staring at the light on the wall. His certainty was immovable; the gentility with which he spoke did not undercut the authority of the statement. "I *belong* to my grandfather. I always have."

"You weren't even born when he—"

"That doesn't matter. Coming and going; that's nothing."

Coming and going, Cleve puzzled. Did Tait mean life and death? He had no chance to ask. Billy was talking again, the same subdued but insistent flow.

"He was guilty, of course. Not the way they thought he was, but *guilty*. He knew what he was and what he was capable of; that's guilt, isn't it? He killed four people. Or at least that's what they hanged him for."

"You mean he killed more?"

Billy made another small shrug: numbers didn't matter apparently. "But nobody came to see where they'd laid him to rest. That's not right, is it? They didn't care, I suppose. All the family were glad he was gone, probably. Thought he was wrong in the head from the beginning. But he wasn't. I know he *wasn't*. I've got his hands, and his eyes. So Mama said. She told me all about him, you see, just before she died. Told me things she'd never told anybody, and only told me because of my eyes..." He faltered, and put his hand to his lip, as if the fluctuating light on the brick had already mesmerized him into saying too much.

"What did your mother tell you?" Cleve pressed him.

Billy seemed to weigh up alternative responses before offering one. "Just that he and I were *alike* in some ways," he said.

"Crazy, you mean?" Cleve said, only half-joking.

"Something like that," Billy replied, eyes still on the wall. He sighed, then allowed himself a further confession. "That's why I came here. So my grandfather would know he hadn't been forgotten."

"Came here?" said Cleve. "What are you talking about? You were caught and sentenced. You had no choice."

The light on the wall was extinguished as a cloud passed over the sun. Billy looked up at Cleve. The light was there, in his eyes.

"I committed a crime to get here," the boy replied. "It was a deliberate act."

Cleve shook his head. The claim was preposterous.

"I tried before—twice. It's taken time. But I got here, didn't I?"

"Don't take me for a fool, Billy," Cleve warned.

"I don't," the other replied. He stood up now. He seemed somehow lighter for the story he'd told; he even smiled, if tentatively, as he said: "You've been good to me. Don't think

I don't know that. I'm grateful. Now"—He faced Cleve before saying—"I want to know where the graves are. Find that out and you won't hear another peep from me, I promise."

•

Cleve knew next to nothing about the prison or its history, but he knew somebody who did. There was a man by the name of Bishop—so familiar with the inmates that his name had acquired the definite article—who was often at the workshop at the same time as Cleve. The Bishop had been in and out of prison for much of his forty-odd years, mostly for misdemeanors, and, with all the fatalism of a one-legged man who makes a life study of monopedia, had become an expert on prisons and the penal system. Little of his information came from books. He had gleaned the bulk of his knowledge from old lags and screws who wanted to talk the hours away, and by degrees he had turned himself into a walking encyclopedia on crime and punishment. He had made it his trade, and he sold his carefully accrued knowledge by the sentence; sometimes as geographical information to the would-be escapee, sometimes as prison mythology to the godless con in search of a local divinity. Now Cleve sought him out and laid down his payment in tobacco and IOUs.

"What can I do for you?" The Bishop asked. He was heavy but not unhealthily so. The needle-thin cigarettes he was perpetually rolling and smoking were dwarfed by his butcher's fingers, stained sepia by nicotine.

"I want to know about the hangings here."

The Bishop smiled. "Such good stories," he said, and began to tell.

On the plain details, Billy had been substantially correct. There had been hangings in Pentonville up until the middle of the century, but the shed had long since been demolished. On the spot now stood the Probation Office in B Wing. As to the story of Crippen's roses, there was truth in that too. In

front of a hut on the grounds, which, The Bishop informed
Cleve, was a store for gardening equipment, was a small patch
of grass, in the center of which a bush flourished, planted (and
at this point The Bishop confessed that he could not tell fact
from fiction) in memory of Doctor Crippen, hanged in 1910.

"That's where the graves are?" Cleve asked.

"No, no," The Bishop said, reducing half of one of his skinny
cigarettes to ash with a single inhalation. "The graves are along-
side the wall, to the left behind the hut. There's a long lawn;
you must have seen it."

"No stones?"

"Absolutely not. The plots have always been left unmarked.
Only the governor knows who's buried where, and he's probably lost the plans." The Bishop ferreted for his tobacco tin in
the breast pocket of his prison-issue shirt and began to roll
another cigarette with such familiarity he scarcely glanced down
at what he was doing. "Nobody's allowed to come and mourn,
you see. Out of sight, out of mind: that's the idea. Of course,
that's not the way it works, is it? People forget prime ministers,
but they remember murderers. You walk on that lawn, and
just six feet under are some of the most notorious men who
ever graced this green and pleasant land. And not even a cross
to mark the spot. Criminal, isn't it?"

"You know who's buried there?"

"Some very wicked gentlemen," The Bishop replied, as if
fondly admonishing them for their mischief mongering.

"You heard of a man called Edgar Tait?"

Bishop raised his eyebrows; the fat of his brow furrowed.
"Saint Tait? Oh certainly. He's not easily forgotten."

"What do you know about him?"

"He killed his wife, and then his children. Took a knife to
them all, as I live and breathe."

"All?"

The Bishop put the freshly rolled cigarette to his thick lips.
"Maybe not all," he said, narrowing his eyes as he tried to

recall the specific details. "Maybe one of them survived. I think perhaps a daughter." He shrugged dismissively. "I'm not very good at remembering the victims. But then, who is?" He fixed his bland gaze on Cleve. "Why are you so interested in Tait? He was hanged before the war."

"Nineteen thirty-seven. He'll be well gone, eh?"

The Bishop raised a cautionary forefinger. "Not so," he said. "You see, the land this prison is built upon has special properties. Bodies buried here don't rot the way they do elsewhere." Cleve shot The Bishop an incredulous glance. "It's true," the fat man protested mildly. "I have it on unimpeachable authority. Take it from me, whenever they've had to exhume a body from the plot it's always been found in almost perfect condition." He paused to light his cigarette and drew upon it, exhaling the smoke through his mouth with his next words. "When the end of the world is upon us, the good men of Marylebone and Camden Town will rise up as rot and bone. But the wicked? They'll dance to Judgment as fresh as the day they dropped. Imagine that." This perverse notion clearly delighted him. His pudgy face puckered and dimpled with pleasure at it. "Ah," he mused, "and who'll be calling who corrupt on *that* fine morning?"

•

Cleve never worked out precisely how Billy talked his way on to the gardening detail, but he managed it. Perhaps he had appealed directly to Mayflower, who'd persuaded his superiors that the boy could be trusted out in the fresh air. However he worked the maneuver, in the middle of the week following Cleve's discovery of the graves' whereabouts, Billy was out in the cold April morning cutting grass.

What happened that day filtered back down the grapevine around recreation time. Cleve had the story from three independent sources, none of whom had been on the spot. The accounts had a variety of colorations, but were clearly of the same species. The bare bones went as follows:

The gardening detail, made up of four men watched over by a single prison guard, were moving around the blocks, trimming grass and weeding beds in preparation for the spring planting. Custody had been lax, apparently. It was two or three minutes before the guard even noticed that one of his charges had edged to the periphery of the party and slipped away. The alarm was raised. The guards did not have to look far, however. Tait had made no attempt to escape, or if he had he'd been stymied in his bid by a fit of some kind, which had crippled him. He was found (and here the stories parted company considerably) on a large patch of lawn beside the wall, lying on the grass. Some reports claimed he was black in the face, his body knotted up and his tongue all but bitten through; others that he was found facedown, talking to the earth, weeping and cajoling. The consensus was that the boy had lost his mind.

The rumors made Cleve the center of attention, a situation he did not relish. For the next day he was scarcely left alone, men wanting to know what it was like to share a cell with a lunatic. He had nothing to tell, he insisted. Tait had been the perfect cell-mate—quiet, undemanding and unquestionably sane. He told the same story to Mayflower when he was grilled the following day, and later, to the prison doctor. He let not a breath of Tait's interest in the graves be known and made it his business to see The Bishop and request a similar silence of him. The man was willing to oblige only if vouchsafed the full story in due course. This Cleve promised. The Bishop, as befitted his assumed clerisy, was as good as his word.

•

Billy was gone for two days. In the interim Mayflower disappeared from his duties as Landing Officer. No explanation was given. In his place a man called Devlin was transferred from D Wing. His reputation went before him. He was not, it seemed, a man of rare compassion. The impression was confirmed when, the day of Billy Tait's return, Cleve was summoned into Devlin's office.

"I'm told you and Tait are close," Devlin said. He had a face as giving as granite.

"Not really, sir."

"I'm not going to make Mayflower's mistake, Smith. As far as I'm concerned, Tait is trouble. I'm going to watch him like a hawk, and when I'm not here you're going to do it for me, understand? If he so much as crosses his eyes it's the ghost train. I'll have him out of here and into a special unit before he can fart. Do I make myself clear?"

"Paying your respects, were you?"

Billy had lost weight in the hospital, pounds his scrawny frame could scarcely afford. His shirt hung off his shoulders; his belt was on its tightest notch. The thinning more than ever emphasized his physical vulnerability; a featherweight blow would floor him, Cleve thought. But it lent his face a new, almost desperate, intensity. He seemed all eyes, and those had lost all trace of captured sunlight. Gone, too, was the pretense of vacuity, replaced with an eerie purposefulness.

"I asked a question."

"I heard you," Billy said. There was no sun today, but he looked at the wall anyway. "Yes, if you must know, I was paying my respects."

"I've been told to watch you, by Devlin. He wants you off the Landing. Transferred entirely, maybe."

"Out?" The panicked look Billy gave Cleve was too naked to be met for more than a few seconds. "Away from here, you mean?"

"I would think so."

"They can't!"

"Oh, they can. They call it the ghost train. One minute you're here; the next—"

"No," the boy said, hands suddenly fists. He had begun to shake, and for a moment Cleve feared a second fit. But he seemed, by act of will, to control the tremors, and turned his look back to his cell-mate. The bruises he'd received from Lowell had dulled to yellow-gray, but far from disappeared; his unshaven cheeks were dusted with pale-ginger hair. Looking at him Cleve felt an unwelcome twinge of concern.

"Tell me," Cleve said.

"Tell you what?" Billy asked.

"What happened at the graves."

"I felt dizzy. I fell over. The next thing I knew I was in hospital."

"That's what you told *them*, isn't it?"

"It's the truth."

"Not the way I heard it. Why don't you explain what really happened? I want you to trust me."

"I do," the boy said. "But I have to keep this to myself, see. It's between me and him."

"You and Edgar?" Cleve asked, and Billy nodded. "A man who killed all his family but your mother?"

Billy was clearly startled that Cleve possessed this information. "Yes," he said after consideration. "Yes, he killed them all. He would have killed Mama too if she hadn't escaped. He wanted to wipe the whole family out. So there'd be no heirs to carry the bad blood."

"Your blood's bad, is it?"

Billy allowed himself the slenderest of smiles. "No," he said. "I don't think so. Grandfather was wrong. Times have changed, haven't they?"

He *is* mad, Cleve thought. Lightning-swift, Billy caught the judgment.

"I'm not insane," he said. "You tell them that. Tell Devlin and whoever else asks. Tell them I'm a lamb." The fierceness was back in his eyes. There was nothing lamblike there, though Cleve forbore saying so. "They mustn't move me out, Cleve.

Not after getting so close. I've got business here. Important business."

"With a dead man?"

"With a dead man."

•

Whatever new purpose he displayed for Cleve, the shutters went up when Billy got back among the rest of the cons. He responded neither to the questions nor the insults bandied about; his facade of empty-eyed indifference was flawless. Cleve was impressed. The boy had a future as an actor, if he decided to forsake professional lunacy.

But the strain of concealing the newfound urgency in him rapidly began to tell. In a hollowness about the eyes and a jitteriness in his movements; in brooding and unshakable silences. The physical deterioration was apparent to the doctor to whom Billy continued to report; he pronounced the boy suffering from depression and acute insomnia and prescribed sedatives to aid sleep. These pills Billy gave to Cleve, insisting he had no need of them himself. Cleve was grateful. For the first time in many months he began to sleep well, unperturbed by the tears and shouts of his fellow inmates.

By day, the relationship between him and the boy, which had always been vestigial, dwindled down to mere courtesy. Cleve sensed that Billy was closing up entirely, removing himself from merely physical concerns.

It was not the first time he had witnessed such a premeditated withdrawal. His sister-in-law, Rosanna, had died of stomach cancer three years earlier: a protracted and, until the last weeks, steady decline. Cleve had not been close to her, but perhaps that very distance had lent him a perspective on the woman's behavior that the rest of his family had lacked. He had been startled at the systematic way she had prepared herself for death, drawing in her affections until they touched only the most vital figures in her life—her children and her priest—and exiling all others, including her husband of fourteen years.

Now he saw the same dispassion and frugality in Billy. Like a man in training to cross a waterless wasteland and too possessive of his energies to squander them in a single fruitless gesture, the boy was sinking into himself. It was eerie; Cleve became increasingly uncomfortable sharing the twelve feet by eight of the cell with Billy. It was like living with a man on Death Row.

The only consolation was the tranquilizers, which Billy readily charmed the doctor into continuing to supply. They guaranteed Cleve sleep that was restful, and, for several days at least, dreamless.

And then he dreamed the city.

Not the city first; first the desert. An empty expanse of blue-black sand, which stung the soles of his feet as he walked, and was blown up by a cool wind into his nose and eyes and hair. He had been here before, he knew. His dream-self recognized the vista of barren dunes, with neither tree nor habitation to break the monotony. But on previous visits he had come with guides (or such was his half-formed belief); now he was alone, and the clouds above his head were heavy and slate-gray, promising no sun. For what seemed hours he walked the dunes, his feet turned bloody by the sharp sand, his body, dusted by the grains, tinged blue. As exhaustion came close to defeating him, he saw ruins and approached them.

It was no oasis. There was nothing in those empty streets of health or sustenance; no fruitful trees nor sparkling fountains. The city was a conglomeration of houses, or parts of same—sometimes entire floors, sometimes single rooms—thrown down side by side in parodies of urban order. The styles were a hopeless mishmash: fine Georgian establishments standing beside mean tenement buildings with rooms burned out; a house plucked from a terraced row, perfect down to the glazed dog on the windowsill, back to back with a penthouse suite. All were scarred by a rough removal from their context: walls

were cracked, offering sly glimpses into private interiors; staircases beetled cloudward without destination; doors flapped open
and closed in the wind, letting on to nowhere.

There was life here, Cleve knew. Not just the lizards, rats
and butterflies—albinos all—that fluttered and skipped in front
of him as he walked the forsaken streets—but *human* life. He
sensed that every step he took was watched over, though he
saw no sign of human presence—not on his first visit, at least.

On the second, his dream-self forsook the trudge across the
wilderness and was delivered directly into the necropolis, his
feet, easily tutored, following the same route as he had on his
first visit. The constant wind was stronger tonight. It caught
the lace curtains in this window, and a tinkling Chinese trinket
hanging in that. It carried voices too; horrid and outlandish
sounds that came from some distant place far beyond the city.
Hearing that whirring and whittering, as of insane children,
he was grateful for the streets and the rooms, for their familiarity
if not for any comfort they might offer. He had no desire to
step into those interiors, voices or no; he did not want to
discover what marked out these snatches of architecture that
they should have been ripped from their roots and flung down
in this whining desolation.

Yet once he had visited the site, his sleeping mind went
back there, night upon night; always walking, bloody-footed,
seeing only the lizards and the rats and the butterflies, and the
black sand on each threshold, blowing into rooms and hallways
that never changed from visit to visit; that seemed, from what
he could glimpse between the curtains or through a shattered
wall, to have been *fixed* somehow at some pivotal moment,
with a meal left uneaten on a table set for three (the capon
uncarved, the sauces steaming), or a shower left running in a
bathroom in which the lamp perpetually swung; and in a room
that might have been a lawyer's study a lapdog, or else a wig
torn off and flung to the floor, lying discarded on a fine carpet
whose intricacies were half devoured by sand.

Only once did he see another human being in the city, and that was Billy. It happened strangely. One night, as he dreamed the streets, he half stirred from sleep. Billy was awake, and standing in the middle of the cell, staring up at the light through the window. It was not moonlight, but the boy bathed in it as if it were. His face was turned up to the window, mouth open and eyes closed. Cleve barely had time to register the trance the boy seemed to be in before the tranquilizers drew him back into his dream. He took a fragment of reality with him however, folding the boy into his sleeping vision. When he reached the city again, there was Billy Tait: standing on the street, his face turned up to the lowering clouds, his mouth open, his eyes closed.

The image lingered only a moment. The next, the boy was away, his heels kicking up black fans of sand. Cleve called after him. Billy ran on however, heedless; and with that inexplicable foreknowledge that dreams bring, Cleve knew where the boy was going. Off to the edge of the city, where the houses petered out and the desert began. Off to meet some friend coming in on that terrible wind, perhaps. Nothing would induce him into pursuit; yet he didn't want to lose contact with the one fellow human he had seen in these destitute streets. He called Billy's name again, more loudly.

This time he felt a hand on his arm, and started up in terror to find himself being jostled awake in his cell.

"It's all right," Billy said. "You're dreaming."

Cleve tried to shake the city out of his head, but for several perilous seconds the dream bled into the waking world, and looking down at the boy he saw Billy's hair lifted by a wind that did not, *could* not, belong in the confines of the cell. "You're dreaming," Billy said again. "Wake up."

Shuddering, Cleve sat fully up on his bunk. The city was receding—was almost gone—but before he lost sight of it entirely he felt the indisputable conviction that Billy *knew* what he was waking Cleve from; that they had been together for a few fragile moments.

"You know, don't you?" he accused the pallid face at his side.

The boy looked bewildered. "What are you talking about?"

Cleve shook his head. The suspicion became more incredible with each step he took from sleep. Even so, when he looked down at Billy's bony hand, which still clung to his arm, he half expected to see flecks of that obsidian grit beneath his fingernails. There was only dirt.

The doubts lingered however, long after reason should have bullied them into surrender. Cleve found himself watching the boy more closely from that night on, waiting for some slip of tongue or eye which would reveal the nature of his game. Such scrutiny was a lost cause. The last traces of accessibility disappeared that night; the boy became—like Rosanna—an indecipherable book, letting no clue as to the nature of his secret world out from beneath his lids. As to the dream—it was not even mentioned again. The only roundabout allusion to that night was Billy's redoubled insistence that Cleve continue to take the sedatives.

"You need your sleep," he said after coming back from the infirmary with a further supply. "Take them."

"You need sleep too," Cleve replied, curious to see how far the boy would push the issue. "I don't need the stuff any more."

"But you do," Billy insisted, proffering the vial of capsules. "You know how bad the noise is."

"Someone said they're addictive," Cleve replied, not taking the pills. "I'll do without."

"*No*," said Billy, and now Cleve sensed a level of insistence which confirmed his deepest suspicions. The boy *wanted* him drugged, and had all along. "I sleep like a babe," Billy said. "Please take them. They'll only be wasted otherwise."

Cleve shrugged. "If you're sure," he said, content—fears confirmed—to make a show of relenting.

"I'm sure."

"Then thanks." He took the vial.

Billy beamed. With that smile, in a sense, the bad times really began.

•

That night, Cleve answered the boy's performance with one of his own, appearing to take the tranquilizers as he usually did but failing to swallow them. Once lying on his bunk, face to the wall, he slipped them from his mouth and under his pillow. Then he pretended sleep.

Prison days both began and finished early; by eight forty-five or nine most of the cells in the four wings were in darkness, the inmates locked up until dawn and left to their own devices. Tonight was quieter than most. The weeper in the next cell but one had been transferred to D Wing; there were few other disturbances along the landing. Even without the pill Cleve felt sleep tempting him. From the bunk below he heard practically no sound, except for the occasional sigh. It was impossible to guess if Billy was actually asleep or not. Cleve kept his silence, occasionally stealing a moment-long glance at the luminous face of his watch. The minutes were leaden, and he feared, as the first hours crept by, that all too soon his imitation of sleep would become the real thing. Indeed he was turning this very possibility around in his mind when unconsciousness overcame him.

He woke much later. His sleep position seemed not to have altered. The wall was in front of him, the peeled paint like a dim map of some nameless territory. It took him a minute or two to orient himself. There was no sound from the bunk below. Disguising the gesture as one made in sleep, he drew his arm up within eye range, and looked at the pale green dial of his watch. It was one fifty-one. Several hours yet until dawn. He lay in the position he'd awakened in for a full quarter of an hour, listening for every sound in the cell, trying to locate

Billy. He was loath to roll over and look for himself, for fear that the boy was standing in the middle of the cell as he had been the night of the visit to the city.

The world, though benighted, was far from silent. He could hear dull footsteps as somebody paced back and forth in the corresponding cell on the landing above; could hear water rushing in the pipes and the sound of a siren on Caledonian Road. What he couldn't hear was Billy. Not a breath of the boy.

Another quarter of an hour passed, and Cleve could feel the familiar torpor closing in to reclaim him; if he lay still much longer he would fall asleep again, and the next thing he'd know it would be morning. If he was going to learn anything, he had to roll over and *look*. Wisest, he decided, not to attempt to move surreptitiously but to turn over as naturally as possible. This he did, muttering to himself, as if in sleep, to add weight to the illusion. Once he had turned completely, and positioned his hand beside his face to shield his spying, he cautiously opened his eyes.

The cell seemed darker than it had the night he had seen Billy with his face up to the window. As to the boy, he was not visible. Cleve opened his eyes a little wider and scanned the cell as best he could from between his fingers. There was something amiss, but he couldn't quite work out what it was. He lay there for several minutes, waiting for his eyes to become accustomed to the murk. They didn't. The scene in front of him remained unclear, like a painting so encrusted with dirt and varnish its depths refuse the investigating eye. Yet he knew—*knew*—that the shadows in the corners of the cell, and on the opposite wall, were not empty. He wanted to end the anticipation that was making his heart thump, wanted to raise his head from the pebble-filled pillow and call Billy out of hiding. But good sense counseled otherwise. Instead he lay still, and sweated, and watched.

And now he began to realize what was wrong with the scene

before him. The concealing shadows fell where no shadows belonged; they spread across the floor where the feeble light from the window should have been falling. Somehow, between window and wall, that light had been choked and devoured. Cleve closed his eyes to give his befuddled mind a chance to rationalize and reject this conclusion. When he opened them again his heart lurched. The shadow, far from losing potency, had grown a little.

He had never been afraid like this before, never felt a coldness in his innards akin to the chill that found him now. It was all he could do to keep his breath even and his hands where they lay. His instinct was to wrap himself up and hide his face like a child. Two thoughts kept him from doing so. One was that the slightest movement might draw unwelcome attention to him. The other, that Billy was somewhere in the cell, and perhaps as threatened by this living darkness as he.

And then, from the bunk below, the boy spoke. His voice was soft, presumably so as not to wake his sleeping cell-mate. It was also eerily intimate. Cleve entertained no thought that Billy was talking in his sleep; the time for willful self-deception was long past. The boy was addressing the darkness; of that unpalatable fact there could be no doubt.

"...it hurts..." he said, with a faint note of accusation. "...You didn't tell me how much it hurts...."

Was it Cleve's imagination, or did the wraith of shadows bloom a little in response, like a squid's ink in water? He was horribly afraid.

The boy was speaking again. His voice was so low Cleve could barely catch the words.

"...it must be soon..." he said with quiet urgency. "...I'm not afraid. Not afraid."

Again the shadow shifted. This time, when Cleve looked into its heart, he made some sense of the chimerical form it embraced. His throat shook; a cry lodged behind his tongue, hot to be shouted.

"... all you can teach me ..." Billy was saying, "... quickly ..." The words came and went, but Cleve barely heard them. His attention was on the curtain of shadow, and the figure—stitched from darkness—that moved in its folds. It was not an illusion. There was a man there: or rather a crude copy of one, its substance tenuous, its outline deteriorating all the time and being hauled back into some semblance of humanity again only with the greatest effort. Of the visitor's features Cleve could see little, but enough to sense deformities paraded like virtues: a face resembling a plate of rotted fruit, pulpy and peeling, swelling here with a nest of flies, and there suddenly fallen away to a pestilent core. How could the boy bring himself to converse so easily with such a *thing*? And yet, putrescence notwithstanding, there was a bitter dignity in the bearing of the creature, in the anguish of its eyes, and the toothless O of its maw.

Suddenly, Billy stood up. The abrupt movement, after so many hushed words, almost unleashed the cry from Cleve's throat. He swallowed it, with difficulty, and closed his eyes down to a slit, staring through the bars of his lashes at what happened next.

Billy was talking again, but now the voice was too low to allow for eavesdropping. He stepped toward the shadow, his body blocking much of the figure on the opposite wall. The cell was no more than two or three strides wide, but by some mellowing of physics, the boy seemed to take five, six, seven steps away from the bunk. Cleve's eyes widened: he knew he was not being watched. The shadow and its acolyte had business between them: it occupied their attention utterly.

Billy's figure was smaller than seemed possible within the confines of the cell, as if he had stepped through the wall and into some other province. And only now, with his eyes wide, did Cleve recognize that place. The darkness from which Billy's visitor was made was cloud-shadow and dust; behind him, barely visible in the bewitched murk, but recognizable to any who had been there, was the city of Cleve's dreams.

Billy had reached his master. The creature towered above him, tattered and spindly, but aching with power. Cleve didn't know how or why the boy had gone to it, and he feared for Billy's safety now that he had, but fear for his own safety shackled him to the bunk. He realized in that moment that he had never loved anyone, man or woman, sufficiently to pursue them into the shadow of that shadow. The thought brought a terrible isolation, knowing that same instant that none, seeing *him* walk to his damnation, would take a single step to claim him from the brink. Lost souls both, he and the boy.

Now Billy's lord was lifting his swollen head, and the incessant wind in those blue streets was rousing his horse mane into furious life. On the wind, the same voices Cleve had heard carried before, the cries of mad children, somewhere between tears and howls. As if encouraged by these voices, the entity reached out toward Billy and embraced him, wrapping the boy round in vapor. Billy did not struggle in his embrace but rather returned it. Cleve, unable to watch this horrid intimacy, closed his eyes against it, and when—seconds? minutes?, later—he opened them again, the encounter seemed to be over. The shadow thing was blowing apart, relinquishing its slender claim to coherence. It fragmented, pieces of its tattered anatomy flying off into the streets like litter before wind. Its departure seemed to signal the dispersal of the entire scene; the streets and houses were already being devoured by dust and distance. Even before the last of the shadow's scraps had been wafted out of sight the city was lost to sight. Cleve was pleased to be rid of it. Reality, grim as it was, was preferable to that desolation. Brick by painted brick the wall was asserting itself again, and Billy, delivered from his master's arms, was back in the solid geometry of the cell, staring up at the light through the window.

Cleve did not sleep again that night. Indeed he wondered,

lying on his unyielding mattress and staring up at the stalactites of paint depending from the ceiling, whether he could ever again find safety in sleep.

•

Sunlight was a showman. It threw its brightness down with such flamboyance, eager as any tinsel-merchant to dazzle and distract. But beneath the gleaming surface it illuminated was another state; one that sunlight—ever the crowd pleaser—conspired to conceal. It was vile and desperate, that condition. Most, blinded by sight, never even glimpsed it. But Cleve knew the state of sunlessness now; had even walked it, in dreams; and though he mourned the loss of his innocence, he knew he could never retrace his steps back into light's hall of mirrors.

•

He tried his damnedest to keep this change in him from Billy; the last thing he wanted was for the boy to suspect his eavesdropping. But concealment was well nigh impossible. Though the following day Cleve made every show of normality he could contrive, he could not quite cover his unease. It slipped out without his being able to control it, like sweat from his pores. And the boy knew, no doubt of it, he *knew*. Nor was he slow to give voice to his suspicions. When, following the afternoon's workshop, they returned to their cell, Billy was quick to come to the point.

"What's wrong with you today?"

Cleve busied himself with remaking his bed, afraid even to glance at Billy. "Nothing's wrong," he said. "I don't feel particularly well, that's all."

"You have a bad night?" the boy inquired. Cleve could feel Billy's eyes boring into his back.

"No," he said, pacing his denial so that it didn't come too quickly. "I took your pills, like always."

"Good."

The exchange faltered, and Cleve was allowed to finish his bed making in silence. The business could only be extended so long, however. When he turned from the bunk, job done, he found Billy sitting at the small table, with one of Cleve's books open in his lap. He casually flicked through the volume, all sign of his previous suspicion vanished. Cleve knew better than to trust to mere appearances, however.

"Why'd you read these things?" the boy asked.

"Passes the time," Cleve replied, undoing all his labors by clambering up on to the top bunk and stretching out there.

"No. I don't mean why do you read books? I mean, why read *these* books? All this stuff about sin."

Cleve only half heard the question. Lying there on the bunk reminded him all too acutely of how the night had been. Reminded him too that darkness was even now crawling up the side of the world again. At that thought his stomach seemed to aspire to his throat.

"Did you hear me?" the boy asked.

Cleve murmured that he had.

"Well, why then; why the books? About damnation and all?"

"Nobody else takes them out of the library," Cleve replied, having difficulty shaping thoughts to speak when the others, unspoken, were so much more demanding.

"You don't believe it then?"

"No," he replied. "No, I don't believe a word of it."

The boy kept his silence for a while. Though Cleve wasn't looking at him, he could hear Billy turning pages. Then, another question, but spoken more quietly; a confession.

"Do you ever get *afraid?*"

The inquiry startled Cleve from his trance. The conversation had changed back from talk of reading matter to something altogether more pertinent. Why did Billy ask about fear unless he too was afraid?

"What have I got to be scared of?" Cleve asked.

From the corner of his eye he caught the boy shrugging slightly before replying. "Things that happen," he said, his voice soulless. "Things you can't control."

"Yes," Cleve replied, not certain of where this exchange was leading. "Yes, of course. Sometimes I'm scared."

"What do you do then?" Billy asked.

"Nothing *to* do, is there?" Cleve said. His voice was as hushed as Billy's. "I gave up praying the morning my father died."

He heard the soft pat as Billy closed the book and inclined his head sufficiently to catch sight of the boy. Billy could not entirely conceal his agitation. He *is* afraid, Cleve saw; he doesn't want the night to come any more than I do. He found the thought of their shared fear reassuring. Perhaps the boy didn't entirely belong to the shadow; perhaps he could even cajole Billy into pointing their route out of this spiraling nightmare.

He sat upright, his head within inches of the cell ceiling. Billy looked up from his meditations, his face a pallid oval of twitching muscle. Now was the time to speak, Cleve knew; *now*, before the lights were switched out along the landings, and all the cells consigned to shadows. There would be no time then for explanations. The boy would already be half lost to the city and beyond persuasion.

"I have dreams," Cleve said. Billy said nothing but simply stared back, hollow-eyed. "I dream a city."

The boy didn't flinch. He clearly wasn't going to volunteer elucidation; he would have to be bullied into it.

"Do you know what I'm talking about?"

Billy shook his head. "No," he said lightly, "I never dream."

"Everybody dreams."

"Then I just don't remember them."

"I remember mine," Cleve said. He was determined, now that he'd broached the subject, not to let Billy squirm free. "And you're there. You're in that city."

Now the boy flinched; only a treacherous lash but enough to reassure Cleve that he wasn't wasting his breath.

"What is that place, Billy?" he asked.

"How should I know?" the boy returned, about to laugh, then discarding the attempt. "I don't know, do I? They're your dreams."

Before Cleve could reply he heard the voice of one of the guards as he moved along the row of cells, telling the men to bed down for the night. Very soon, the lights would be extinguished and he would be locked up in this narrow cell for ten hours. With Billy; and phantoms.

"Last night," he said, fearful of mentioning what he'd heard and seen without due preparation, but more fearful still of facing another night on the borders of the city, alone in darkness. "Last night I saw..." He faltered. Why wouldn't the words come? "Saw..."

"Saw what?" the boy demanded, his face inscrutable; whatever sign of apprehension there had been in it had now vanished. Perhaps he too had heard the guard's advance and known that there was nothing to be done; no way of staying the night's advance.

"What did you see?" Billy insisted.

Cleve sighed. "My mother," he replied.

The boy betrayed his relief only in the tenuous smile that crept across his lips.

"Yes... I saw my mother. Large as life."

"And it upset you, did it?" Billy asked.

"Sometimes dreams do."

The guard had reached B. 3. 20. "Lights out in two minutes," he said as he passed.

"You should take some more of those pills," Billy advised, putting down the book and crossing to his bunk. "Then you'd be like me. No dreams."

Cleve had lost. He, the arch bluffer, had been outbluffed by the boy, and now had to take the consequences. He lay, facing the ceiling, counting off the seconds until the light went out, while below the boy undressed and slipped between the sheets.

There was still time to jump up and call the guard back; time to beat his head against the door until somebody came. But what would he say to justify his histrionics? That he had bad dreams? *Who didn't?* That he was afraid of the dark? *Who wasn't?* They would laugh in his face and tell him to go back to bed, leaving him with all camouflage blown, and the boy and his master waiting at the wall. There was no safety in such tactics.

Nor in prayer either. He had told Billy the truth, about his giving up God when his prayers for his father's life had gone unanswered. Of such divine neglect was atheism made; belief could not be rekindled now, however profound his terror.

Thoughts of his father led inevitably to thoughts of childhood; few other subjects, if any, could have engrossed his mind sufficiently to steal him from his fears but this. When the lights were finally extinguished, his frightened mind took refuge in memories. His heart rate slowed; his fingers ceased to tremble, and eventually, without his being the least aware of it, sleep stole him.

The distractions available to his conscious mind were not available to his unconscious. Once asleep, fond recollection was banished; childhood memories became a thing of the past, and he was back, bloody-footed, in that terrible city.

Or rather, on its borders. For tonight he did not follow the familiar route past the Georgian house and its attendant tenements, but walked instead to the outskirts of the city, where the wind was stronger than ever, and the voices it carried clear. Though he expected with every step he took to see Billy and his dark companion, he saw nobody. Only butterflies accompanied him along the path, luminous as his watch face. They settled on his shoulders and his hair like confetti, then fluttered off again.

He reached the edge of the city without incident and stood, scanning the desert. The clouds, solid as ever, moved overhead with the majesty of juggernauts. The voices seemed closer tonight, he thought, and the passions they expressed less distressing than he had found them previously. Whether the mellowing was in them or in his response to them he couldn't be certain.

And then, as he watched the dunes and the sky, mesmerized by their blankness, he heard a sound and glanced over his shoulder to see a smiling man, dressed in what was surely his Sunday finery, walking out of the city toward him. He was carrying a knife; the blood on it, and on his hand and shirt front, was wet. Even in his dream state, and immune, Cleve was intimidated by the sight and stepped back—a word of self-defense on his lips. The smiling man seemed not to see him however, but advanced past Cleve and out into the desert, dropping the blade as he crossed some invisible boundary. Only now did Cleve see that others had done the same, and that the ground at the city limit was littered with lethal keepsakes—knives, ropes (even a human hand, lopped off at the wrist)—most of which were all but buried.

The wind was bringing the voices again: tatters of senseless songs and half-finished laughter. He looked up from the sand. The exiled man had gone out a hundred yards from the city and was now standing on top of one of the dunes, apparently waiting. The voices were becoming louder all the time. Cleve was suddenly nervous. Whenever he had been here in the city, and heard this cacophony, the picture he had conjured of its originators had made his blood run cold. Could he now stand and wait for the banshees to appear? Curiosity was discretion's better. He glued his eyes to the ridge over which they would come, his heart thumping, unable to look away. The man in the Sunday suit had begun to take his jacket off. He discarded it and began to loosen his tie.

And now Cleve thought he saw something in the dunes,

and the noise rose to an ecstatic howl of welcome. He stared, defying his nerves to betray him, determined to look this horror in its many faces.

Suddenly, above the din of their music, somebody was screaming; a man's voice, but high-pitched, gelded with terror. It did not come from here in the dream-city, but from that other fiction he occupied, the name of which he couldn't quite remember. He pressed his attention back to the dunes, determined not to be denied the sight of the reunion about to take place in front of him. The scream in that nameless elsewhere mounted to a throat-breaking height, and stopped. But now an alarm bell was ringing in its place, more insistent than ever. Cleve could feel his dream slipping.

"No..." he murmured, "...let me see...."

The dunes were moving. But so was his consciousness— out of the city and back toward his cell. His protests brought him no concession. The desert faded, the city too. He opened his eyes. The lights in the cell were still off: the alarm bell was ringing. There were shouts in cells on the landings above and below, and the sound of guards' voices, raised in a confusion of inquiries and demands.

He lay on his bunk a moment, hoping, even now, to be returned into the enclave of his dream. But no; the alarm was too shrill, the mounting hysteria in the cells around too compelling. He conceded defeat and sat up, wide awake.

"What's going on?" he said to Billy.

The boy was not standing in his place by the wall. Asleep, for once, despite the din.

"*Billy?*"

Cleve leaned over the edge of his bunk, and peered into the space below. It was empty. The sheets and blankets had been thrown back.

Cleve jumped down from his bunk. The entire contents of the cell could be taken at two glances, there was nowhere to hide. The boy was not to be seen. Had he been spirited away

while Cleve slept? It was not unheard of; this was the ghost
train of which Devlin had warned: the unexplained removal
of difficult prisoners to other establishments. Cleve had never
heard of this happening at night, but there was a first time for
everything.

He crossed to the door to see if he could make some sense
of the shouting outside, but it defied interpretation. The likeliest explanation was a fight, he suspected: two cons who could
no longer bear the idea of another hour in the same space.
He tried to work out where the initial scream had come from,
to his right or left, above or below; but the dream had confounded all direction.

As he stood at the door, hoping a guard might pass by, he
felt a change in the air. It was so subtle he scarcely registered
it at first. Only when he raised his hand to wipe sleep from
his eyes did he realize that his arms were solid gooseflesh.

From behind him he now heard the sound of breathing, or
a ragged parody of same.

He mouthed the word "Billy" but didn't speak it. The gooseflesh had found his spine; now he began to shake. The cell
wasn't empty after all; there was somebody in the tiny space
with him.

He screwed his courage tight and forced himself to turn
around. The cell was darker than it had been when he awoke;
the air was a teasing veil. But Billy was not in the cell; nobody
was.

And then the noise came again and drew Cleve's attention
to the bottom bunk. The space was pitch black, a shadow—
like that on the wall—too profound and too volatile to have
natural origins. Out of it, a croaking attempt at breath that
might have been the last moments of an asthmatic. He realized
that the murk in the cell had its source there—in the narrow
space of Billy's bed; the shadow bled onto the floor and curled
up like fog on to the top of the bunk.

Cleve's supply of fear was not inexhaustible. In the past

several days he had used it up in dreams and waking dreams; he'd sweated, he'd frozen, he'd lived on the edge of sane experience and survived. Now, though his body still insisted on gooseflesh, his mind was not moved to panic. He felt cooler than he ever had, whipped by recent events into a new impartiality. He would *not* cower. He would *not* cover his eyes and pray for morning, because if he did one day he would wake to find himself dead and he'd never know the nature of this mystery.

He took a deep breath and approached the bunk. It had begun to shake. The shrouded occupant in the lower tier was moving about violently.

"Billy," Cleve said.

The shadow moved. It pooled around his feet; it rolled up into his face, smelling of rain on stone, cold and comfortless.

He was standing no more than a yard from the bunk, and still he could make nothing out; the shadow defied him. Not to be denied sight, he reached toward the bed. At his solicitation the veil divided like smoke, and the shape that thrashed on the mattress made itself apparent.

It was Billy, of course; and yet not. A lost Billy, perhaps, or one to come. If so, Cleve wanted no part of a future that could breed such trauma. There, on the lower bunk, lay a dark, wretched shape, still solidifying as Cleve watched, knitting itself together from the shadows. There was something of a rabid fox in its incandescent eyes, in its arsenal of needle-teeth; something of an upturned insect in the way it was half curled upon itself, its back more shell than flesh and more nightmare than either. No part of it was fixed. Whatever figuration it had (perhaps it had many) Cleve was watching the status dissolve. The teeth were growing yet longer and, in so doing, more insubstantial, their matter extruded to the point of frailty, then dispersed like mist; its hooked limbs, pedaling the air, were also growing paltry. Beneath the chaos he saw the ghost of Billy Tait, mouth open and babbling agonies, striving to make itself known. He wanted to reach into the maelstrom and snatch the boy out, but he sensed that the process he was watching had its own momentum and it might be fatal to intervene. All he could do was stand and watch as Billy's thin white limbs and heaving abdomen writhed to slough off this dire anatomy. The luminous eyes were almost the last to go, spilling out from their sockets on myriad threads and flying off into black vapor.

At last he saw Billy's face, truant clues to its former condition still flickering across it. And then, even these were dispersed, the shadows gone, and only Billy was lying on the bunk, naked and heaving with the exertion of his anguish.

He looked at Cleve, his face innocent of expression.

Cleve remembered how the boy had complained to the creature from the city. "... *it hurts* ... " he'd said, hadn't he? "... *You didn't tell me how much it hurts*. ..." It was the observable truth. The boy's body was a wasteland of sweat and bone; a more unappetizing sight was scarcely imaginable. But *human*; at least that.

Billy opened his mouth. His lips were ruddy and slick, as if he were wearing lipstick.

"Now ... ," he said, trying to speak between painful breaths. "Now what shall we do?"

The act of speaking seemed too much for him. He made a gagging sound in the back of his throat, and pressed his hand to his mouth. Cleve moved aside as Billy stood up and stumbled across to the bucket in the corner of the cell, kept there for their night wastes. He failed to reach it before nausea overtook him; fluid splashed between his fingers and hit the floor. Cleve looked away as Billy threw up, preparing himself for the stench he would have to tolerate until slopping-out time the following morning. It was not the smell of vomit that filled the cell, however, but something sweeter and more cloying.

Mystified, Cleve looked back toward the figure crouching in the corner. On the floor between his feet were splashes of dark fluid; rivulets of the same ran down his bare legs. Even in the gloom of the cell, it was unmistakably blood.

·

In the most well-ordered of prisons violence could—and inevitably did—erupt without warning. The relationship of two cons, incarcerated together for sixteen hours out of every twenty-four, was an unpredictable thing. But as far as had been apparent to either prisoners or guards there had been no bad blood between Lowell and Nayler; nor, until that scream began, had there been a sound from their cell: no argument, no raised voices. What had induced Nayler to spontaneously attack and slaughter his cell-mate, and then inflict devastating wounds upon himself, was a subject for debate in dining hall and exercise yard alike. The why of the problem, however, took second place to the how. The rumors describing the condition of Lowell's body when found defied the imagination; even among men inured against casual brutality the descriptions were met with shock. Lowell had not been much liked; he had been a bully and a cheat. But nothing he'd done deserved such mutilation. The man had been ripped open, his eyes put out, his genitals torn off. Nayler, the only possible antagonist, had then contrived to open up his own belly. He was now in an intensive care unit; the prognosis was not hopeful.

·

It was easy, with such a buzz of outrage going about the wing, for Cleve to spend the day all but unnoticed. He too had a story to tell: but who would believe it? He barely believed it himself. In fact on and off through the day, when the images came back to him afresh, he asked himself if he was entirely sane. But then sanity was a movable feast, wasn't it? One man's madness might be another's politics. All he knew for certain was that he had seen Billy Tait transform. He clung to that certainty with a tenaciousness born of near despair. If he ceased to believe the evidence of his own eyes, he had no defense left to hold the darkness at bay.

After ablutions and breakfast, the entire wing was confined to cells; workshops, recreation—any activity that required movement around the landings—was canceled while Lowell's cell was photographed and examined, then swabbed out. Following breakfast, Billy slept through the morning; a state more akin to coma than sleep, such was its profundity. When he awoke for lunch he was brighter and more outgoing than Cleve had seen him in weeks. There was no sign beneath the vacuous chatter that he knew what had happened the previous night. In the afternoon Cleve faced him with the truth.

"You killed Lowell," he said. There was no point in trying to pretend ignorance any longer; if the boy didn't remember now what he'd done, he would surely recall in time. And with that memory, how long before he remembered that Cleve had watched him transform? Better to confess it now. "I saw you," Cleve said. "I saw you change. . . ."

Billy didn't seem much disturbed by these revelations.

"Yes," he said. "I killed Lowell. Do you blame me?" The question, begging a hundred others, was put lightly, as a matter of mild interest, no more.

"What happened to you?" Cleve said. "I saw you—*there*"— he pointed, appalled at the memory, at the lower bunk—"you weren't human."

"I didn't mean you to see," the boy replied. "I gave you the pills, didn't I? You shouldn't have spied."

"And the night before . . . ," Cleve said. "I was awake then too."

The boy blinked like a bemused bird, head slightly cocked. "You really have been stupid," he said. "So stupid."

"Whether I like it or not, I'm not out of this," Cleve said. "I have dreams."

"Oh, yes." Now a frown marred the porcelain brow. "Yes. You dream the city, don't you?"

"What is that place, Billy?"

"I read somewhere: *The dead have highways.* You ever hear that? Well... they have cities too."

"The dead? You mean it's some kind of ghost town?"

"I never wanted you to become involved. You've been better to me than most here. But I *told* you, I came to Pentonville to do business."

"With Tait."

"That's right."

Cleve wanted to laugh; what he was being told—*a city of the dead?*—only heaped nonsense upon nonsense. And yet his exasperated reason had not sniffed out one explanation more plausible.

"My grandfather killed his children," Billy said, "because he didn't want to pass his condition on to another generation. He learned late, you see. He didn't realize, until he had a wife and children, that he wasn't like most men. He was special. But he didn't *want* the skills he'd been given, and he didn't want his children to survive with that same power in their blood. He would have killed himself, and finished the job, but that my mother escaped. Before he could find her and kill her too, he was arrested."

"And hanged. And buried."

"Hanged and buried, but not *lost.* Nobody's lost, Cleve. Not ever."

"You came here to find him."

"More than find him: make him *help* me. I knew from the age of ten what I was capable of. Not quite consciously, but I had an inkling. And I was afraid. Of course I was afraid: it was a terrible mystery."

"This mutation: you've always done it?"

"No. Only *known* I was capable of it. I came here to make

my grandfather tutor me, make him *show me how.* Even now"—
he looked down at his wasted arms—"with him teaching me
. . . the pain is almost unbearable."

"Why do it then?"

The boy looked at Cleve incredulously. "To be *not* myself;
to be smoke and shadow. To be something terrible." He seemed
genuinely puzzled by Cleve's unwillingness. "Wouldn't you
do the same?"

Cleve shook his head. "What you became last night was
repellent."

Billy nodded. "That's what my grandfather thought. At his
trial he called himself an abomination. Not that they knew
what he was talking about, of course, but that's what he said.
He stood up and said: 'I am Satan's excrement'"—Billy smiled
at the thought—"'for God's sake hang me and burn me.' He's
changed his mind since then. The century's getting old and
stale; it needs new tribes." He looked at Cleve intently. "Don't
be afraid," he said. "I won't hurt you, unless you try to tell
tales. You won't do that, will you?"

"What could I say that would sound like sanity?" Cleve
returned mildly. "No, I won't tell tales."

"Good. And in a little while I'll be gone, and you'll be gone.
And you can forget."

"I doubt it."

"Even the dreams will stop when I'm not here. You only
share them because you have some mild talents as a sensitive.
Trust me. There's nothing to be afraid of."

"The city—"

"What about it?"

"Where are its citizens? I never see anybody. No, that's not
quite true. I saw one. A man with a knife . . . going out into
the desert . . ."

"I can't help you. I go as a visitor myself. All I know is what
my grandfather tells me: that it's a city occupied by dead souls.

Whatever you've seen there, forget about it. You don't belong there. You're not dead yet."

•

Was it wise to believe always what the dead told you? Were they purged of all deceit by the act of dying, and delivered into their new state like saints? Cleve could not believe such naiveté. More likely they took their talents with them, good and bad, and used them as best they could. There would be shoemakers in paradise, wouldn't there? Foolish to think they'd forgotten how to sew leather.

So perhaps Edgar Tait *lied* about the city. There was more to that place than Billy knew. What about the voices on the wind, the man and the knife, dropping it among a litter of weapons before moving off to God alone knew where? What ritual was that?

Now—with the fear used up, and no untainted reality left to cling to, Cleve saw no reason not to go to the city willingly. What could be there, in those dusty streets, that was worse than what he had seen in the bunk below him, or what had happened to Lowell and Nayler? Beside such atrocities the city was a haven. There was a serenity in its empty thoroughfares and plazas; a sense Cleve had there that all action was over, all rage and distress finished with; that these interiors (with the bath running and the cup brimming) had seen the *worst*, and were now content to sit out the millennium. When that night brought sleep, and the city opened up in front of him, he went into it not as a frightened man astray in hostile territory but as a visitor content to relax a while in a place he knew too well to become lost in, but not well enough to be weary of.

As if in response to this newfound ease, the city opened itself to him. Wandering the streets, feet bloody as ever, he found the doors open wide, the curtains at the windows drawn back. He did not disparage the invitation they offered but went to look more closely at the houses and tenements. On closer inspection he found them not the paradigms of domestic calm he'd first taken them for. In each he discovered some sign of violence recently done. In one, perhaps no more than an overturned chair, or a mark on the floor where a heel had slid in a spot of blood; in others, the manifestations were more obvious. A hammer, its claw clotted, had been left on a table laid with newspapers. There was a room with its floorboards ripped up, and black plastic parcels, suspiciously slick, laid beside the hole. In one, a mirror had been shattered; in another, a set of false teeth left beside a hearth in which a fire flared and spat.

They were murder scenes, all of them. The victims had gone—to other cities, perhaps, full of slaughtered children and murdered friends—leaving these tableaux fixed forever in the breathless moments that followed the crime. Cleve walked down the streets, the perfect voyeur, and peered into scene after scene, reconstructing in his mind's eye the hours that had preceded the studied stillness of each room. Here a child had died: its cot was overturned; here someone had been murdered in his bed, the pillow soaked in blood; the ax on the carpet. Was this damnation then, the killers obliged to wait out some portion of eternity (all of it, perhaps) in the room they had murdered in?

Of the malefactors themselves he saw nothing, though logic implied that they must be close by. Was it that they had the power of invisibility to keep themselves from the prying eyes of touring dreamers like himself; or did a time in this nowhere transform them, so that they were no longer flesh and blood but became part of their cell—a chair, a china doll?

Then he remembered the man at the perimeter who'd come in his fine suit, bloody-handed, and walked out into the desert. *He* had not been invisible.

"Where are you?" he said, standing on the threshold of a

mean room, with an open oven and utensils in the sink, water running on them. "Show yourself."

A movement caught his eye, and he glanced across to the door. There was a man standing there. He had been there all along, Cleve realized, but so still, and so perfectly a part of this room, that he had not been visible until he moved his eyes and looked Cleve's way. He felt a twinge of unease, thinking that each room he had peered into had, most likely, contained one or more killers, each similarly camouflaged by stasis. The man, knowing he'd been seen, stepped out of hiding. He was in late middle-age and had cut himself that morning as he shaved.

"Who are you?" he said. "I've seen you before. Walking by."

He spoke softly and sadly—an unlikely killer, Cleve thought.

"Just a visitor," he told the man.

"There are no visitors here," he replied, "only prospective citizens."

Cleve frowned, trying to work out what the man meant. But his dream-mind was sluggish, and before he could solve the riddle of the man's words there were others.

"Do I know you?" the man asked. "I find I forget more and more. That's no use, is it? If I forget I'll never leave, will I?"

"Leave?" Cleve repeated.

"Make an exchange," the man said, realigning his toupee.

"And go where?"

"Back. Do it over."

Now he approached Cleve across the room. He stretched out his hands, palms up; they were blistered.

"You can help me," he said. "I can make a deal with the best of them."

"I don't understand you."

The man clearly thought he was bluffing. His upper lip, which boasted a dyed black mustache, curled. "Yes you do," he said. "You understand perfectly. You just want to sell yourself, the way everybody does. Highest bidder, is it? What are you, an assassin?"

Cleve shook his head. "I'm just dreaming," he replied.

The man's fit of pique subsided. "Be a friend," he said. "I've got no influence; not like some. Some of them, you know, they come here and they're out again in a matter of hours. They're professionals. They make arrangements. But me? With me it was a crime of passion. I didn't come prepared. I'll stay here till I can make a deal. Please be a friend."

"I can't help you," Cleve said, not even certain of what the man was requesting.

The killer nodded. "Of course not," he said, "I didn't expect..."

He turned from Cleve and moved to the oven. Heat flared up from it and made a mirage of the hob. Casually, he put one of his blistered palms on the door and closed it; almost as soon as he had done so it creaked open again. "Do you know just how appetizing it is—the smell of cooking flesh?" he said, as he returned to the oven door and attempted to close it a second time. "Can anybody blame me? Really?"

Cleve left him to his ramblings; if there was sense there it was probably not worth his laboring over. The talk of exchanges and of escape from the city: it defied Cleve's comprehension.

He wandered on, tired now of peering into the houses. He'd seen all he wanted to see. Surely morning was close, and the bell would ring on the landing. Perhaps he should even wake himself, he thought, and be done with this tour for the night.

As the thought occurred, he saw the girl. She was no more than six or seven years old, and she was standing at the next intersection. This was no killer, surely. He started toward her. She, either out of shyness or some less benign motive, turned to her right and ran off. Cleve followed. By the time he had reached the intersection she was already a long way down the next street; again he gave chase. As dreams would have such pursuits, the laws of physics did not pertain equally to pursuer and pursued. The girl seemed to move easily, while Cleve struggled against air as thick as treacle. He did not give up, however, but pressed on wherever the girl led. He was soon a good distance from any location he recognized in a warren of yards and alleyways—all, he supposed, scenes of blood-letting. Unlike the main thoroughfares, this ghetto contained few entire spaces, only snatches of geography: a grass verge, more red than green; a piece of scaffolding, with a noose depending from it; a pile of earth. And now, simply, a wall.

The girl had led him into a cul-de-sac; she herself had disappeared however, leaving him facing a plain brick wall, much weathered, with a narrow window in it. He approached: this was clearly what he'd been led here to see. He peered through the reinforced glass, dirtied on his side by an accumulation of bird-droppings, and found himself staring into one of the cells at Pentonville. His stomach flipped over. What kind of game was this; led out of a cell and into this dream-city, only to be led back into prison? But a few seconds of study told him that it was not *his* cell. It was Lowell and Nayler's. Theirs were the pictures taped to the gray brick, theirs the blood spread over floor and wall and bunk and door. This was another murder scene.

"My God Almighty," he murmured. "Billy..."

He turned away from the wall. In the sand at his feet lizards were mating; the wind that found its way into this backwater brought butterflies. As he watched them dance, the bell rang in B Wing, and it was morning.

·

It was a trap. Its mechanism was by no means clear to Cleve—but he had no doubt of its purpose. Billy would go to the city, soon. The cell in which he had committed murder already awaited him, and of all the wretched places Cleve had seen in that assemblage of charnel houses surely the tiny, blood-drenched cell was the worst.

The boy could not know what was planned for him; his grandfather had lied about the city by exclusion, failing to tell Billy what special qualifications were required to exist there. And why? Cleve returned to the oblique conversation he'd had with the man in the kitchen. That talk of exchanges, of deal making, of *going back*. Edgar Tait had regretted his sins, hadn't he? He'd decided, as the years passed, that he was *not* the Devil's excrement, that to be returned into the world would not be so bad an idea. Billy was somehow an instrument in that return.

"My grandfather doesn't like you," the boy said when they were locked up again after lunch. For the second consecutive day all recreation and workshop activities had been canceled, while a cell-by-cell inquiry was undertaken regarding Lowell's and—as of the early hours of that day—Nayler's deaths.

"Doesn't he?" Cleve said. "And why?"

"Says you're too inquisitive. In the city."

Cleve was sitting on the top bunk; Billy on the chair against the opposite wall. The boy's eyes were bloodshot; a small but constant tremor had taken over his body.

"You're going to die," Cleve said. What other way to state that fact was there, but baldly? "I saw . . . in the city . . ."

Billy shook his head. "Sometimes you talk like a crazy man. My grandfather says I shouldn't trust you."

"He's afraid of me, that's why."

Billy laughed derisively. It was an ugly sound, learned, Cleve guessed, from Grandfather Tait. "He's afraid of no one," Billy retorted.

"Afraid of what I'll see. Of what I'll tell you."

"No," said the boy with absolute conviction.

"He told you to kill Lowell, didn't he?"

Billy's head jerked up. "Why'd you say that?"

"You never wanted to murder him. Maybe scare them both

a bit, but not *kill* them. It was your loving grandfather's idea."

"Nobody tells me what to do," Billy replied, his gaze icy. "Nobody."

"All right," Cleve conceded, "maybe he *persuaded* you, eh? Told you it was a matter of family pride. Something like that?" The observation clearly touched a nerve; the tremors had increased.

"So? What if he did?"

"I've seen where you're going to go, Billy. A place just waiting for you." The boy stared at Cleve but didn't interrupt. "Only murderers occupy the city, Billy. That's why your grandfather's there. And if he can find a replacement—if he can reach out and make more murder—he can go free."

Billy stood up, face like a fury. All trace of derision had gone. "What do you mean *free?*"

"Back to the world. *Back here.*"

"You're lying."

"Ask him."

"He wouldn't cheat me. His blood's my blood."

"You think he cares? After fifty years in that place, waiting for a chance to be out and away. You think he gives a *damn* how he does it?"

"I'll tell him how you lie," Billy said. The anger was not entirely directed at Cleve; there was an undercurrent of doubt there, which Billy was trying to suppress. "You're dead," he said, "when he finds out how you're trying to poison me against him. You'll see him, then. Oh yes. You'll see him. And you'll wish to Christ you hadn't."

·

There seemed to be no way out. Even if Cleve could convince the authorities to move him before night fell—(a slim chance indeed; he would have to reverse all that he had claimed about the boy, tell them Billy was dangerously insane, or something similar. Certainly not the truth.)—even if he were to have himself transferred to another cell, there was no promise of safety in such a maneuver. The boy had said he was smoke and shadow. Neither door nor bars could keep such insinuations at bay; the fate of Lowell and Nayler was proof positive of that. Nor was Billy alone. There was Edgar St. Clair Tait to be accounted for, and what powers might he possess? Yet to stay in the same cell with the boy tonight would amount to self-slaughter, wouldn't it? He would be delivering himself into the hands of the beasts.

When they left their cells for the evening meal, Cleve looked around for Devlin, located him, and asked for the opportunity of a short interview, which was granted. After the meal, Cleve reported to the officer.

"You asked me to keep an eye on Billy Tait, sir."

"What about him?"

Cleve had thought hard about what he might tell Devlin that would bring an immediate transfer: nothing had come to mind. He stumbled, hoping for inspiration, but was empty-mouthed.

"I . . . I . . . want to put in a request for a cell transfer."

"Why?"

"The boy's unbalanced," Cleve replied. "I'm afraid he's going to do me harm. Have another of his fits."

"You could lay him flat with one hand tied behind your back. He's worn to the bone." At this point, had he been talking to Mayflower, Cleve might had been able to make a direct appeal to the man. With Devlin such tactics would be doomed from the beginning.

"I don't know why you're complaining. He's been as good as gold," said Devlin, savoring the parody of fond father. "Quiet; always polite. He's no danger to you or anyone."

"You don't know him—"

"What are you trying to pull?"

"Put me in a Rule 43 cell, sir. *Anywhere*, I don't mind. Just get me out of his way. *Please*."

Devlin didn't reply but stared at Cleve, mystified. At last, he said, "You *are* afraid of him."

"Yes."

"What's wrong with you? You've shared cells with hard men and never turned a hair."

"He's different," Cleve replied; there was little else he could say except: "He's insane. I tell you he's insane."

"All the world's crazy, save thee and me, Smith. Hadn't you heard?" Devlin laughed. "Go back to your cell and stop bellyaching. You don't want a ghost train ride, now do you?"

•

When Cleve returned to the cell, Billy was writing a letter. Sitting on his bunk, poring over the paper, he looked utterly vulnerable. What Devlin said was true: the boy *was* worn to the bone. It was difficult to believe, looking at the ladder of his vertebrae, visible through his T-shirt, that this frail form could survive the throes of transformation. But then, maybe it would not. Maybe the rigors of change would tear him apart with time. But not soon enough.

"Billy . . ."

The boy didn't take his eyes from his letter.

". . . what I said, about the city . . ."

He stopped writing—

". . . Maybe I *was* imagining it all. Just dreaming."

—and started again.

". . . I only told you because I was afraid for you. That was all. I want us to be friends."

Billy looked up. "It's not in my hands," he said very simply. "Not now. It's up to Grandfather. He may be merciful; he may not."

"Why do you have to tell him?"

"He knows what's in me. He and I . . . we're like one. That's how I know he wouldn't cheat me."

Soon it would be night; the lights would go out along the wing, the shadows would come.

"So I just have to wait, do I?" Cleve said.

Billy nodded. "I'll call him, and then we'll see."

Call him? Cleve thought. Did the old man need summoning from his resting place every night? Was that what he had seen Billy doing, standing in the middle of the cell, eyes closed and face up to the window? If so, perhaps the boy could be *prevented* from putting in his call to the dead.

As the evening deepened Cleve lay on his bunk and thought his options through. Was it better to wait here and see what judgment came from Tait, or attempt to take control of the situation and block the old man's arrival? If he did so, there would be no going back; no room for pleas or apologies: his aggression would undoubtedly breed aggression. If he failed to prevent the boy from calling Tait, it would be the end.

The lights went out. In cells up and down the five landings of B Wing men would be turning their faces to their pillows. Some, perhaps, would lie awake planning their careers when this minor hiccup in their professional lives was over; others would be in the arms of invisible mistresses. Cleve listened to the sounds of the cell: the rattling progress of water in the pipes, the shallow breathing from the bunk below. Sometimes it seemed that he had lived a second lifetime on this stale pillow, marooned in darkness.

The breathing from below soon became practically inaudible; nor was there sound of movement. Perhaps Billy was waiting for Cleve to fall asleep before he made any move. If so, the boy would wait in vain. He would not close his eyes and leave them to slaughter him in his sleep. He wasn't a pig, to be taken uncomplaining to the knife.

Moving as cautiously as possible, so as to arouse no suspicion, Cleve unbuckled his belt and pulled it through the loops of his trousers. He might make a more adequate binding by tearing up his sheet and pillowcase, but he could not do so without arousing Billy's attention. Now he waited, belt in hand, and pretended sleep.

Tonight he was grateful that the noise in the Wing kept stirring him from dozing, because it was fully two hours before Billy moved out of his bunk, two hours in which—despite his fear of what would happen should he sleep—Cleve's eyelids betrayed him on three or four occasions. But others on the landings were tearful tonight; the deaths of Lowell and Nayler had made even the toughest cons jittery. Shouts—and countercalls from those awakened—punctuated the hours. Despite the fatigue in his limbs, sleep did not master him.

When Billy finally got up from the lower bunk it was well past twelve and the landing was all but quiet. Cleve could hear the boy's breath; it was no longer even but had a catch in it. He watched, eyes like slits, as Billy crossed the cell to his familiar place in front of the window. There was no doubt that he was about to call up the old man.

As Billy closed his eyes, Cleve sat up, threw off his blanket and slipped down from the bunk. The boy was slow to respond. Before he quite comprehended what was happening, Cleve had crossed the cell and thrust him back against the wall, hand clamped over Billy's mouth.

"No, you don't," Cleve growled. "I'm not going to go like Lowell." Billy struggled, but Cleve was easily his physical superior.

"He's not going to come tonight," Cleve said, staring into the boy's wide eyes, "because you're not going to call him."

Billy fought more violently to be free, biting hard against his captor's palm. Cleve instinctively removed his hand and in two strides the boy was at the window, reaching up. In his throat, a strange half-song; on his face, sudden and inexplicable tears. Cleve dragged him away.

"Shut your noise up!" he snapped. But the boy continued to make the sound. Cleve hit him, open-handed but hard, across the face. *"Shut up!"* he said. Still the boy refused to cease his singing; now the music had taken on another rhythm. Again Cleve hit him, and again. But the assault failed to silence him. There was a whisper of change in the air of the cell, a shifting in its chiaroscuro. The shadows were moving.

Panic took Cleve. Without warning he made a fist and punched the boy hard in the stomach. As Billy doubled up an upper-cut caught his jaw. It drove his head back against the wall, his skull connecting with the brick. Billy's legs gave and he collapsed. A featherweight, Cleve had once thought, and it was true. Two good punches and the boy was laid out cold.

Cleve glanced around the cell. The movement in the shadows had been arrested; they trembled though, like greyhounds awaiting release. Heart hammering, he carried Billy back to his bunk and laid him down. There was no sign of consciousness returning; the boy lay limply on the mattress while Cleve tore up his sheet and gagged him, thrusting a ball of fabric into the boy's mouth to prevent him from making a sound behind his gag. He then proceeded to tie Billy to the bunk, using both his own belt and the boy's, supplemented with further makeshift bindings of torn sheets. It took several minutes to finish the job. As Cleve was lashing the boy's legs together, Billy began to stir. His eyes flickered open, full of puzzlement. Then, realizing his situation, he began to thrash his head from side to side; there was little else he could do to signal his protest.

"No, Billy," Cleve murmured to him, throwing a blanket across his bound body to keep the fact from any guard who might look in through the peephole before morning, "tonight, you don't bring him. Everything I said was true, boy. He wants out, and he's using you to escape." Cleve took hold of Billy's head, fingers pressed against his cheeks. "He's not your friend. *I am*. Always have been." Billy tried to shake his head from Cleve's grip but couldn't. "Don't waste your energy," Cleve advised. "It's going to be a long night."

He left the boy on the bunk, crossed the cell to the wall, and slid down it to sit on his haunches and watch. He would stay awake until dawn, and then, when there was some light to think by, he'd work out his next move. For now, he was content that his crude tactics had worked.

The boy had stopped trying to fight; he had clearly realized the bonds were too expertly tied to be loosened. A kind of calm descended on the cell: Cleve sitting in the patch of light that fell through the window, the boy lying in the gloom of the lower bunk, breathing steadily through his nostrils. Cleve glanced at his watch. It was twelve fifty-four. When was morning? He didn't know. Five hours, at least. He put his head back, and stared at the light.

It mesmerized him. The minutes ticked by slowly but steadily, and the light did not change. Sometimes a guard would advance along the landing, and Billy, hearing the footsteps, would begin his struggling afresh. But nobody looked into the cell. The two prisoners were left to their thoughts; Cleve to wonder if there would ever come a time when he could be free of the shadow behind him, Billy to think whatever thoughts came to bound monsters. And still the dead-of-night minutes went, minutes that crept across the mind like dutiful school-children, one upon the heels of the next, and after sixty had passed that sum was called an hour. And dawn was closer by that span, wasn't it? But then so was death, and so, presumably, the end of the world: that glorious Last Trump of which The Bishop had spoken so fondly, when the dead men under the lawn outside would rise as fresh as yesterday's bread and go out to meet their Maker. And sitting there against the wall, listening to Billy's inhalations and exhalations, and watching the light in the glass and through the glass, Cleve knew without doubt that even if he escaped this trap, it was only a temporary respite; that this long night, its minutes, its hours, were a foretaste of a longer vigil. He almost despaired then; felt his soul sink into a hole from which there seemed to be no hope of retrieval. *Here* was the real world; he wept. Not joy, not light, not looking forward; only this waiting in ignorance, without hope, even of fear, for fear came only to those with dreams to lose. The hole was deep and dim. He peered up out of it at the light through the window, and his thoughts became one wretched round. He forgot the bunk and the boy lying there. He forgot the numbness that had overtaken his legs. He might, given time, have forgotten even the simple act of taking breath but for the smell of urine that pricked him from his fugue.

He looked toward the bunk. The boy was voiding his bladder, but that act was simply a symptom of something else altogether. Beneath the blanket, Billy's body was moving in a dozen ways that his bonds should have prevented. It took Cleve a few moments to shake off lethargy, and seconds more to realize what was happening. Billy was changing.

Cleve tried to stand upright, but his lower limbs were dead from sitting still for so long. He almost fell forward across the cell, and only prevented himself by throwing out an arm to grasp the chair. His eyes were glued to the gloom of the lower bunk. The movements were increasing in scale and complexity. The blanket was pitched off. Beneath it Billy's body was already beyond recognition; the same terrible procedure as he had seen before, but in reverse. Matter gathering in buzzing clouds about the body, and congealing into atrocious forms. Limbs and organs summoned from the ineffable, teeth shaping themselves like needles and plunging into place in a head grown large and swelling still. He begged for Billy to stop, but with every drawn breath there was less of humanity to appeal to. The strength the boy had lacked was granted to the beast; it had already broken almost all its constraints, and now, as Cleve watched, it struggled free of the last, and rolled off the bunk onto the floor of the cell.

Cleve backed off toward the door, his eyes scanning Billy's mutated form. He remembered his mother's horror at earwigs and saw something of that insect in this anatomy: the way it bent its shiny back upon itself, exposing the paddling intra-cacies that lined its abdomen. Elsewhere, no analogy offered a hold on the sight. Its head was rife with tongues, that licked its eyes clean in place of lids, and ran back and forth across its teeth, wetting and rewetting them constantly; from seeping holes along its flanks came a sewer stench. Yet even now there was a residue of something human trapped in this foulness, its rumor only serving to heighten the filth of the whole. Seeing its hooks and its spines, Cleve remembered Lowell's rising scream and felt his own throat pulse, ready to loose a sound its equal should the beast turn on him.

But Billy had other intentions. He moved—limbs in horrible array—to the window and clambered up, pressing his head against the glass like a leech. The music he made was not like his previous song—but Cleve had no doubt it was the same summoning. He turned to the door and began to beat upon it, hoping that Billy would be too distracted with his call to turn on him before assistance came.

"Quick! For Christ's sake! Quick!" He yelled as loudly as exhaustion would allow, and glanced over his shoulder once to see if Billy was coming for him. He was not; he was still clamped to the window, though his call had all but faltered. Its purpose was achieved. Darkness was tyrant in the cell.

Panicking, Cleve turned back to the door and renewed his tattoo. There was somebody running along the landing now; he could hear shouts and imprecations from other cells. "Jesus Christ, help me!" he shouted. He could feel a chill at his back. He didn't need to turn to know what was happening behind him. The shadow growing, the wall dissolving so that the city and its occupant could come through. Tait was here. He could feel the man's presence, vast and dark. Tait the child killer, Tait the shadow-thing, Tait the transformer. Cleve beat on the door till his hands bled. The feet seemed a continent away. Were they coming? Were they coming?

The chill behind him became a blast. He saw his shadow

thrown up on to the door by flickering blue light; smelled sand
and blood.

And then, the voice. Not the boy, but that of his grandfather,
of Edgar St. Clair Tait. This was the man who had pronounced
himself the Devil's excrement, and hearing that abhorrent
voice, Cleve believed both in hell and its master, believed
himself already in the bowels of Satan, a witness to its wonders.

"You are too inquisitive," Edgar said. "It's time you went
to bed."

Cleve didn't want to turn. The last thought in his head was
that he *should* turn and look at the speaker. But he was no
longer subject to his own will; Tait had fingers in his head and
was dabbling there. He turned, and looked.

The hanged man was in the cell. He was not that beast
Cleve had half seen, that face of pulp and eggs. He was here
in the flesh; dressed for another age, and not without charm.
His face was well made; his brow wide, his eyes unflinching.
He still wore his wedding ring on the hand that stroked Billy's
bowed head like that of a pet dog.

"Time to die, Mr. Smith," he said.

On the landing outside, Cleve heard Devlin shouting. He
had no breath left to answer with. But he heard keys in the
lock or was that some illusion his mind had made to placate
his panic?

The tiny cell was full of wind. It threw over the chair and
table, and lifted the sheets into the air like childhood ghosts.
And now it took Tait, and the boy with him; sucked them back
into the receding perspectives of the city.

"Come on now," Tait demanded, his face corrupting, "we
need you, body and soul. Come with us, Mr. Smith. We
won't be denied."

"No!" Cleve yelled back at his tormentor. The suction was
plucking at his fingers, at his eyeballs. "I won't—"

Behind him, the door was rattling.

"I won't, you hear!"

Suddenly, the door was thrust open, and threw him forward into the vortex of fog and dust that was sucking Tait and his grandchild away. He almost went with them but for a hand that grabbed at his shirt and dragged him back from the brink, even as consciousness gave itself up.

Somewhere, far away, Devlin began to laugh like a hyena. He's lost his mind, Cleve decided; and the image his darkening thoughts evoked was one of the contents of Devlin's brain escaping through his mouth like a flock of flying dogs.

•

He awoke in dreams; and in the city. He awoke remembering his last conscious moments: Devlin's hysteria, the hand arresting his fall as the two figures were sucked away in front of him. He had followed them, it seemed, unable to prevent his comatose mind from retreading the familiar route to the murderers' metropolis. But Tait had not won yet. He was still only *dreaming* his presence here. His corporeal self was still in Pentonville; his dislocation from it informed his every step.

He listened to the wind. It was eloquent as ever: the voices coming and going with each gritty gust, but never, even when the wind died to a whisper, disappearing entirely. As he listened he heard a shout. In this mute city the sound was a shock; it startled rats from their nests and birds up from some secluded plaza.

Curious, he pursued the sound, whose echoes were almost traced on the air. As he hurried down the empty streets he heard further raised voices, and now men and women were appearing at the doors and windows of their cells. So many faces, and nothing in common between one and the next to confirm the hopes of a physiognomist. Murder had as many faces as it had occurrences. The only common quality was one of wretchedness, of minds despairing after an age at the site of their crime. He glanced at them as he went, sufficiently distracted by their looks not to notice where the shout was leading him until he found himself once more in the ghetto to which he had been led by the child.

Now he rounded a corner, and at the end of the cul-de-sac he'd seen from his previous visit here (the wall, the window, the bloody chamber beyond) he saw Billy, writhing in the sand at Tait's feet. The boy was half himself and half that beast he had become in front of Cleve's eyes. The better part was convulsing in its attempt to climb free of the other, but without success. In one moment the boy's body would surface, white and frail, only to be subsumed the next into the flux of transformation. Was that an arm forming, and being snatched away again before it could gain fingers?; was that a face pressed from the house of tongues that was the beast's head? The sight defied analysis. As soon as Cleve fixed upon some recognizable feature it was drowned again.

Edgar Tait looked up from the struggle in front of him, and bared his teeth at Cleve. It was a display a shark might have envied.

"He doubted me, Mr. Smith," the monster said, "and came looking for his cell."

A mouth appeared from the patchwork on the sand and gave out a sharp cry, full of pain and terror.

"Now he wants to be away from me," Tait said. "You sowed the doubt. He must suffer the consequences." He pointed a trembling finger at Cleve, and in the act of pointing the limb transformed, flesh becoming bruised leather. "You came where you were not wanted, and look at the agonies you've brought."

Tait kicked the thing at his feet. It rolled over on to its back, vomiting.

"He needs me," Tait said. "Don't you have the sense to see that? Without me, he's lost."

Cleve didn't reply to the hanged man but instead addressed the beast on the sand.

"Billy?" he said, calling the boy out of the flux.

"Lost," Tait said.

"Billy," Cleve repeated. "Listen to me...."

"He won't go back now," Tait said. "You're just dreaming this. But he's *here*, in the flesh.

"*Billy*," Cleve persevered. "Do you hear me? It's me; it's Cleve."

The boy seemed to pause in its gyrations for an instant, as if hearing the appeal. Cleve said Billy's name again, and again.

It was one of the first skills the human child learned: to call itself something. If anything could reach the boy it was surely his own name.

"Billy... Billy..." At the repeated word, the body rolled itself over.

Tait seemed to have become uneasy. The confidence he'd displayed was now silenced. His body was darkening, the head becoming bulbous. Cleve tried to keep his eyes off the subtle distortions in Edgar's anatomy and concentrate on winning Billy back. The repetition of the name was paying dividends; the beast was being subdued. Moment by moment there was more of the boy emerging. He looked pitiful; skin-and-bones on the black sand. But his face was almost reconstructed now, and his eyes were on Cleve.

"Billy... ?"

He nodded. His hair was plastered to his forehead with sweat; his limbs were in a spasm.

"You know where you are? *Who* you are?"

At first it seemed as though comprehension escaped the boy. And then—by degrees—recognition formed in his eyes, and with it came a terror of the man standing over him.

Cleve glanced up at Tait. In the few seconds since he had last looked all but a few human characteristics had been erased from his head and upper torso, revealing corruptions more profound than those of his grandchild. Billy gazed up over his shoulder like a whipped dog.

"*You belong to me*," Tait pronounced, through features barely capable of speech. Billy saw the limbs descending to snatch at him, and rose from his prone position to escape them, but he was too late. Cleve saw the spiked hook of Tait's limb wrap itself around Billy's neck, and draw him close. Blood leapt from the slit windpipe, and with it the whine of escaping air.

Cleve yelled.

"With me," Tait said, the words deteriorating into gibberish.

Suddenly the narrow cul-de-sac was filling up with brightness, and the boy and Tait and the city were being bleached out. Cleve tried to hold on to them, but they were slipping from him; and in their place another concrete reality: a light, a face (faces) and a voice calling him out of one absurdity and into another.

The doctor's hand was on his face. It felt clammy.

"What on earth were you dreaming about?" he asked, the perfect idiot.

•

Billy had gone.

Of all the mysteries that the governor—and Devlin and the other guards who had stepped into cell B. 3. 20 that night— had to face, the total disappearance of William Tait from an unbreached cell was the most perplexing. Of the vision that had set Devlin giggling like a loon nothing was said; easier to believe in some collective delusion than that they'd seen some objective reality. When Cleve attempted to articulate the events of that night, and of the many nights previous to that, his monologue, interrupted often by his tears and silences, was met with feigned understanding and sideways glances. He told the story over several times, however, despite their condescension, and they, looking no doubt for a clue among his lunatic fables as to the reality of Billy Tait's Houdini act, attended every word. When they found nothing among his tales to advance their investigations, they began to lose their tempers with him. Consolation was replaced with threats. They demanded, voices louder each time they asked the question, where Billy had gone. Cleve answered the only way he knew how. "To the city," he told them. "He's a murderer, you see."

"And his body?" the governor said. "Where do you suppose his *body* is?"

Cleve didn't know, and said so. It wasn't until much later, four full days later in fact, that he was standing by the window watching the gardening detail bearing this spring's plantings cross between wings, that he remembered the lawn.

He found Mayflower, who had been returned to B Wing in lieu of Devlin, and told the officer the thought that had come to him. "He's in the grave," he said. "He's with his grandfather. Smoke and shadow."

They dug up the coffin by cover of night, an elaborate shield of poles and tarpaulins erected to keep proceedings from prying eyes, and lamps, bright as day but not so warm, trained on the labors of the men volunteered as an exhumation party. Cleve's answer to the riddle of Tait's disappearance had met with almost universal bafflement, but no explanation—however absurd—was being overlooked in a mystery so intractable. Thus they gathered at the unmarked grave to turn earth that looked not to have been disturbed in five decades: the governor, a selection of Home Office officials, a pathologist and Devlin. One of the doctors, believing that Cleve's morbid delusion would be best countered if he viewed the contents of the coffin and saw his error with his own eyes, convinced the governor that Cleve should also be numbered among the spectators.

There was little in the confines of Edgar St. Clair Tait's coffin that Cleve had not seen before. The corpse of the murderer—returned here (as smoke perhaps?) neither quite beast nor quite human, and preserved, as The Bishop had promised, as undecayed as the day of his execution—shared the coffin with Billy Tait, who lay, naked as a babe, in his grandfather's embrace. Edgar's corrupted limb was still wound around Billy's neck, and the walls of the coffin were dark with congealed blood. But Billy's face was not besmirched. *He looks like a doll*, one of the doctors observed. Cleve wanted to reply that no doll had such tear stains on its cheeks, nor such despair in its eyes, but the thought refused to become words.

•

Cleve was released from Pentonville three weeks later after special application to the Parole Board, with only two-thirds of his sentence completed. He returned, within half a year, to the only profession that he had ever known. Any hope he might have had of release from his dreams was short-lived. The place was with him still: neither so focused nor so easily traversed now that Billy—whose mind had opened that door—was gone, but still a potent terror, the lingering presence of which wearied Cleve.

Sometimes the dreams would almost recede completely, only to return again with terrible potency. It took Cleve several months before he began to grasp the pattern of this vacillation. *People* brought the dream to him. If he spent time with somebody who had murderous intentions, the city came back. Nor were such people so rare. As he grew more sensitive to the lethal streak in those around him he found himself scarcely able to walk the street. They were *everywhere*, these embryonic killers, people wearing smart clothes and sunny expressions were striding the pavement and imagining, as they strode, the deaths of their employers and their spouses, of soap-opera stars and incompetent tailors. The world had murder on its mind, and he could no longer bear its thoughts.

Only heroin offered some release from the burden of experience. He had never done much intravenous H, but it rapidly became heaven and earth to him. It was an expensive addiction however, and one which his increasingly truncated circle of professional contacts could scarcely hope to finance. It was a man called Grimm, a fellow addict so desperate to avoid reality he could get high on fermented milk, who sug-

gested that Cleve might want to do some work to earn him a
fee the equal of his appetite. It seemed like a wise idea. A
meeting was arranged, and a proposal put. The fee for the job
was so high it could not be refused by a man so in need of
money. The job, of course, was murder.

"There are no visitors here, only prospective citizens." He had
been told that once, though he no longer quite remembered
by whom, and he believed in prophecies. If he didn't commit
murder now, it would only be a matter of time until he did.

But though the details of the assassination that he undertook
had a terrible familiarity to him, he had not anticipated the
collision of circumstances by which he ended fleeing from the
scene of his crime barefoot, and running so hard on pavement
and tarmac that by the time the police cornered him and shot
him down his feet were bloody, and ready at last to tread the
streets of the city—just as he had in dreams.

The room he'd killed in was waiting for him, and he lived
there, hiding his head from any who appeared in the street
outside, for several months. (He assumed time passed here,
by the beard he'd grown; though sleep came seldom, and day
never.) After a while, however, he braved the cool wind and
the butterflies and took himself off to the city perimeters, where
the houses petered out and the desert took over. He went, not
to see the dunes, but to listen to the voices that came always,
rising and falling, like the howls of jackals or children.

He stayed there a long while, and the wind conspired with
the desert to bury him. But he was not disappointed with the
fruit of his vigil. For one day (or year), he saw a man come
to the place and drop a gun in the sand, then wander out into
the desert, where, after a while, the makers of the voices came
to meet him, loping and wild, dancing on their crutches. They
surrounded him, laughing. He went with them, laughing. And
though distance and the wind smudged the sight, Cleve was
certain he saw the man picked up by one of the celebrants,

and taken on to its shoulders as a boy, thence snatched into another's arms as a baby, until, at the limit of his senses, he heard the man bawl as he was delivered back into life. He went away content, knowing at last how sin (and he) had come into the world.

THE

FORBIDDEN

L IKE A FLAWLESS TRAGEDY, THE ELEGANCE OF WHICH
structure is lost upon those suffering in it, the perfect geometry of the Spector Street Estate was visible only from the
air. Walking in its drear canyons, passing through its grimy
corridors from one gray concrete rectangle to the next, there
was little to seduce the eye or stimulate the imagination. What
few saplings had been planted in the quadrangles had long
since been mutilated or uprooted; the grass, though tall, res-
olutely refused a healthy green.

No doubt the estate and its two companion developments
had once been an architect's dream. No doubt the city planners
had wept with pleasure at a design that housed three and thirty-
six persons per hectare, and still boasted space for a children's
playground. Doubtless fortunes and reputations had been built
upon Spector Street, and at its opening fine words had been
spoken of its being a yardstick by which all future developments
would be measured. But the planners—tears wept, words spoken—had left the estate to its own devices; the architects occupied restored Georgian houses at the other end of the city,
and probably never set foot here.

They would not have been shamed by the deterioration of
the estate even if they had. Their brainchild (they would doubtless argue) was as brilliant as ever: its geometries as precise, its
ratios as calculated; it was *people* who had spoiled Spector
Street. Nor would they have been wrong in such an accusation.
Helen had seldom seen an inner city environment so comprehensively vandalized. Lamps had been shattered and backyard fences overthrown; cars whose wheels and engines had
been removed and chassis then burned, blocked garage facilities. In one courtyard three or four ground-floor maisonettes

had been entirely gutted by fire, their windows and doors boarded up with planks and corrugated metal shutters.

More startling still were the graffiti. That was what she had come here to see, encouraged by Archie's talk of the place, and she was not disappointed. It was difficult to believe, staring at the multiple layers of designs, names, obscenities and dogmas that were scrawled and sprayed on every available brick, that Spector Street was barely three and a half years old. The walls, so recently virgin, were now so profoundly defaced that the Council Cleaning Department could never hope to return them to their former condition. A layer of whitewash to cancel this visual cacophony would only offer the scribes a fresh and yet more tempting surface on which to make their mark.

Helen was in seventh heaven. Every corner she turned offered some fresh material for her thesis: "Graffiti: The Semiotics of Urban Despair." It was a subject that married her two favorite disciplines—sociology and esthetics—and as she wandered around the estate she began to wonder if there wasn't a book, in addition to her thesis, in the subject. She walked from courtyard to courtyard, copying down a large number of the more interesting scrawlings and noting their location. Then she went back to the car for her camera and tripod and returned to the most fertile of the areas, to make a thorough visual record of the walls.

It was a chilly business. She was not an expert photographer, and the late October sky was in full flight, shifting the light on the bricks from one moment to the next. As she adjusted and readjusted the exposure to compensate for the light changes, her fingers steadily became clumsier, her temper correspondingly thinner. But she struggled on, the idle curiosity of passersby notwithstanding. There were so many designs to document. She reminded herself that her present discomfort would be amply repaid when she showed the slides to Trevor, whose doubt of the project's validity had been perfectly apparent from the beginning.

"The writing on the wall?" he'd said, half smiling in that irritating fashion of his. "It's been done a hundred times."

This was true, of course; and yet not. There certainly were learned works on graffiti, chock full of sociological jargon: *cultural disenfranchisement; urban alienation*. But she flattered herself that *she* might find something among this litter of scrawlings that previous analysts had not: some unifying convention perhaps, that she could use as the lynchpin of her thesis. Only a vigorous cataloguing and cross-referencing of the phrases and images before her would reveal such a correspondence; hence the importance of this photographic study. So many hands had worked here; so many minds left their mark, however casually: if she could find some pattern, some predominant motive, or *motif*, the thesis would be guaranteed some serious attention, and so, in turn, would she.

"What are you doing?" a voice from behind her asked.

She turned from her calculations to see a young woman with a stroller on the pavement behind her. She looked weary, Helen thought, and pinched by the cold. The child in the stroller was mewling, his grimy fingers clutching an orange lollipop and the wrapping from a chocolate bar. The bulk of the chocolate, and the remains of previous Jujubes, were displayed down the front of his coat.

Helen offered a thin smile to the woman; she looked in need of it.

"I'm photographing the walls," she said in answer to the initial inquiry, though surely this was perfectly apparent.

The woman—she could barely be twenty, Helen judged—said, "You mean the filth?"

"The writing and the pictures," Helen said. Then: "Yes. The filth."

"You from the council?"

"No, the university."

"It's bloody disgusting," the woman said. "The way they do that. It's not just kids, either."

"No?"

"Grown men. Grown men, too. They don't give a damn. Do it in broad daylight. You see 'em . . . broad daylight." She glanced down at the child, who was sharpening his lollipop on the ground. "Kerry!" she snapped, but the boy took no notice. "Are they going to wipe it off?" she asked Helen.

"I don't know," Helen said, and reiterated: "I'm from the university."

"Oh," the woman replied, as if this were new information, "so you're nothing to do with the council?"

"No."

"Some of it's obscene, isn't it. Really dirty. Makes me embarrassed to see some of the things they draw."

Helen nodded, casting an eye at the boy in the stroller. Kerry had decided to put his lollipop in his ear for safekeeping.

"Don't do that!" his mother told him, and leaned over to slap the child's hand. The blow, which was negligible, started the child bawling. Helen took the opportunity to return to her camera. But the woman still desired to talk. "It's not just on the outside, neither," she commented.

"I beg your pardon?" Helen said.

"They break into the flats when they get vacant. The council tried to board them up, but it does no good. They break in anyway. Use them as toilets, and write more filth on the walls. They light fires too. Then nobody can move back in."

The description piqued Helen's curiosity. Would the graffiti on the *inside* walls be substantially different from the public displays? It was certainly worth an investigation.

"Are there any places you know of around here like that?"

"Empty flats, you mean?"

"With graffiti."

"Just by us, there's one or two," the woman volunteered. "I'm in Butts's Court."

"Maybe you could show me?" Helen asked.

The woman shrugged.

"By the way, my name's Helen Buchanan."

"Anne-Marie," the mother replied.

"I'd be very grateful if you could point me to one of those empty flats."

Anne-Marie was baffled by Helen's enthusiasm and made no attempt to disguise it, but she shrugged again and said, "There's nothing much to see. Only more of the same stuff."

Helen gathered up her equipment and they walked side by side through the intersecting corridors between one square and the next. Though the estate was low-rise, each court only five stories high, the effect of each quadrangle was horribly claustrophobic. The walkways and staircases were a thief's dream, rife with blind corners and ill-lit tunnels. The rubbish-dumping facilities—chutes from the upper floors down which bags of refuse could be pitched—had long since been sealed up, thanks to their efficiency as fire traps. Now plastic bags of refuse were piled high in the corridors, many torn open by roaming dogs, their contents strewn across the ground. The smell, even in the cold weather, was unpleasant. In high summer it must have been overpowering.

"I'm over the other side," Anne-Marie said, pointing across the quadrangle. "The one with the yellow door." She then pointed along the opposite side of the court. "Five or six maisonettes from the far end," she said. "There's two of them been emptied out. Few weeks now. One of the family's moved into Ruskin Court; the other did a bunk in the middle of the night."

With that, she turned her back on Helen and wheeled Kerry, who had taken to trailing spittle from the side of his stroller, around the side of the square.

"Thank you," Helen called after her. Anne-Marie glanced over her shoulder briefly but did not reply. Appetite whetted, Helen made her way along the row of ground floor maisonettes, many of which, though inhabited, showed little sign of being so. Their curtains were closely drawn; there were no milk bottles on the doorsteps, or children's toys left where they had been played with. Nothing, in fact, of *life* here. There *were* more graffiti however, sprayed, shockingly, on the doors of occupied houses. She granted the scrawlings only a casual perusal, in part because she feared that one of the doors might open as she examined a choice obscenity sprayed upon it, but more because she was eager to see what revelations the empty flats ahead might offer.

The malign scent of urine, both fresh and stale, welcomed her at the threshold of number 14, and beneath that the smell of burned paint and plastic. She hesitated for fully ten seconds, wondering if stepping into the maisonette was a wise move. The territory of the estate behind her was indisputably foreign, sealed off in its own misery, but the rooms in front of her were more intimidating still: a dark maze which her eyes could barely penetrate. But when her courage faltered she thought of Trevor, and how badly she wanted to silence his condescension. So thinking, she advanced into the place, deliberately kicking a piece of charred timber aside as she did so, in the hope that she would alert any tenant into showing himself.

There was no sound of occupancy however. Gaining confidence, she began to explore the front room of the maisonette which had been—to judge by the remains of a disemboweled sofa in one corner and the sodden carpet underfoot—a living room. The pale green walls were, as Anne-Marie had promised, extensively defaced, both by minor scribblers—content to work in pen, or even more crudely in soft charcoal—and by those with aspirations to public works, who had sprayed the walls in half a dozen colors.

Some of the comments were of interest, though many she had already seen on the walls outside. Familiar names and couplings repeated themselves. Though she had never set eyes on these individuals she knew how badly Fabian J. (A OK!) wanted to deflower Michelle; and that Michelle, in her turn, had the hots for somebody called Mr. Sheen. Here, as elsewhere, a man called White Rat boasted of his endowment, and the return of the Syllabub Brothers was promised in red paint. One or two of the pictures accompanying, or at least adjacent to, these phrases were of particular interest. An almost emblematic simplicity informed them. Beside the word *Christos* was a stick man with his hair radiating from his head like spines, and other heads impaled on each spine. Close by was an image of intercourse so brutally reduced that at first Helen took it to illustrate a knife plunging into a sightless eye. But fascinating as the images were, the room was too gloomy for her film and she had neglected to bring a flash. If she wanted a reliable record of these discoveries she would have to come again and for now be content with a simple exploration of the premises.

The maisonette wasn't that large, but the windows had been boarded up throughout, and as she moved farther from the front door the dubious light petered out altogether. The smell of urine, which had been strong at the door, intensified too, until by the time she reached the back of the living room and stepped along a short corridor into another room beyond, it was as cloying as incense. This room, being farthest from the front door, was also the darkest, and she had to wait a few moments in the cluttered gloom to allow her eyes to become useful. This, she guessed, had been the bedroom. What little furniture the residents had left behind them had been smashed to smithereens. Only the mattress had been left relatively untouched, dumped in the corner of the room among a wretched litter of blankets, newspapers and pieces of crockery.

Outside, the sun found its way between the clouds, and two or three shafts of sunlight slipped between the boards nailed across the bedroom window and pierced the room like annunciations, scoring the opposite wall with bright lines. Here, the graffitists had been busy once more: the usual clamor of love letters and threats. She scanned the wall quickly, and as she did so her eye was led by the beams of light across the room to the wall that contained the door she had stepped through.

Here, the artists had also been at work, but had produced an image the like of which she had not seen anywhere else. Using the door, which was centrally placed in the wall like a mouth, the artists had sprayed a single, vast head onto the stripped plaster. The painting was more adroit than most she had seen, rife with detail that lent the image an unsettling veracity. The cheekbones jutting through skin the color of buttermilk; the teeth, sharpened to irregular points, all converging on the door. The sitter's eyes were, owing to the room's low ceiling, set mere inches above the upper lip, but this physical adjustment only lent force to the image, giving the impression that he had thrown his head back. Knotted strands of his hair snaked from his scalp across the ceiling.

Was it a portrait? There was something naggingly *specific* in the details of the brows and the lines around the wide mouth; in the careful picturing of those vicious teeth. A nightmare certainly: a facsimile, perhaps, of something from a heroin fugue. Whatever its origins, it was potent. Even the illusion of door-as-mouth worked. The short passageway between living room and bedroom offered a passable throat, with a tattered lamp in lieu of tonsils. Beyond the gullet, the day burned white in the nightmare's belly. The whole effect brought to mind a ghost train painting. The same heroic deformity, the same unashamed intention to scare. And it worked; she stood in the bedroom almost stupefied by the picture, its red-rimmed eyes fixing her mercilessly. Tomorrow, she determined, she would come here again, this time with high-speed film and a flash to illuminate the masterwork.

As she prepared to leave the sun went in, and the bands of light faded. She glanced over her shoulder at the boarded windows, and saw for the first time that one four-word slogan had been sprayed on the wall beneath them.

"Sweets to the sweet," it read. She was familiar with the quote, but not with its source. Was it a profession of love? If so, it was an odd location for such an avowal. Despite the mattress in the corner, and the relative privacy of this room, she could not imagine the intended reader of such words ever stepping in here to receive her bouquet. No adolescent lovers, however heated, would lie down here to play at mothers and fathers; not under the gaze of the terror on the wall. She crossed to examine the writing. The paint looked to be the same shade of pink as had been used to color the gums of the screaming man; perhaps the same hand?

Behind her, a noise. She turned so quickly she almost tripped over the blanket-strewn mattress.

"Who—?"

At the other end of the gullet, in the living room, was a scab-kneed boy of six or seven. He stared at Helen, eyes glittering in the half-light, as if waiting for a cue.

"Yes?" she said.

"Anne-Marie says do you want a cup of tea?" he declared without pause or intonation.

Her conversation with the woman seemed hours past. She was grateful for the invitation however. The damp in the maisonette had chilled her.

"Yes..." she said to the boy. "Yes please."

The child didn't move but simply stared at her.

"Are you going to lead the way?" she asked him.

"If you want," he replied, unable to raise a trace of enthusiasm.

"I'd like that."

"You taking photographs?" he asked.

"Yes. Yes, I am. But not in here."

"Why not?"

"It's too dark," she told him.

"Don't it work in the dark?" he wanted to know.

"No."

The boy nodded at this, as if the information somehow fitted well into his scheme of things, and about-turned without another word, clearly expecting Helen to follow.

•

If she had been taciturn in the street, Anne-Marie was anything but in the privacy of her own kitchen. Gone was the guarded curiosity, to be replaced by a stream of lively chatter and a constant scurrying between half a dozen minor domestic tasks, like a juggler keeping several plates spinning simultaneously. Helen watched this balancing act with some admiration; her own domestic skills were negligible. At last, the meandering conversation turned back to the subject that had brought Helen here.

"Them photographs," Anne-Marie said, "why'd you want to take them?"

"I'm writing about graffiti. The photos will illustrate my thesis."

"It's not very pretty."

"No, you're right, it isn't. But I find it interesting."

Anne-Marie shook her head. "I hate the whole estate," she said. "It's not safe here. People getting robbed on their own doorsteps. Kids setting fire to the rubbish day in, day out. Last summer we had the fire brigade here two, three times a day, till they sealed them chutes off. Now people just dump the bags in the passageways, and that attracts rats."

"Do you live here alone?"

"Yes," she said, "since Davey walked out."

"That your husband?"

"He was Kerry's father, but we weren't never married. We lived together two years, you know. We had some good times. Then he just upped and went off one day when I was at me Mam's with Kerry." She peered into her tea cup. "I'm better off without him," she said. "But you get scared sometimes. Want some more tea?"

"I don't think I've got time."

"Just a cup," Anne-Marie said, already up and unplugging the electric kettle to take it to the sink for a refill. As she was about to turn on the tap she saw something on the draining board and drove her thumb down, grinding it out. "Got you, you bugger," she said, then turned to Helen. "We got these bloody ants."

"Ants?"

"Whole estate's infected. From Egypt, they are: pharaoh ants, they're called. Little brown sods. They breed in the central heating ducts, you see; that way they get into all the flats. Place is plagued with them."

This unlikely exoticism (ants from Egypt?) struck Helen as comical, but she said nothing. Anne-Marie was staring out of the kitchen window and into the backyard.

"You should tell them," she said, though Helen wasn't certain whom she was being instructed to tell. "Tell them that ordinary people can't even walk the streets any longer—"

"Is it really so bad?" Helen said, frankly tiring of this catalogue of misfortunes.

Anne-Marie turned from the sink and looked at her hard.

"We've had murders here," she said.

"Really?"

"We had one in the summer. An old man he was, from Ruskin. That's just next door. I didn't know him, but he was a friend of the sister of the woman next door. I forget his name."

"And he was murdered?"

"Cut to ribbons in his own front room. They didn't find him for almost a week."

"What about his neighbors? Didn't they notice his absence?"

Anne-Marie shrugged, as if the most important pieces of information—the murder and the man's isolation—had been divulged and any further inquiries into the problem were irrelevant. But Helen pressed the point.

"Seems strange to me," she said.

Anne-Marie plugged in the filled kettle. "Well, it happened," she replied, unmoved.

"I'm not saying it didn't, I just—"

"His eyes had been taken out," she said, before Helen could voice any further doubts.

Helen winced. "No," she said under her breath.

"That's the truth," Anne-Marie said. "And that wasn't all that'd been done to him." She paused for effect, then went on: "You wonder what kind of person's capable of doing things like that, don't you? You wonder." Helen nodded. She was thinking precisely the same thing.

"Did they ever find the man responsible?"

Anne-Marie snorted her disparagement: "Police don't give a damn what happens here. They keep off the estate as much as possible. When they do patrol all they do is pick up kids for getting drunk and that. They're afraid, you see. That's why they keep clear."

"Of this killer?"

"Maybe," Anne-Marie replied. Then: "He had a hook."

"A hook?"

"The man what done it. He had a hook, like Jack the Ripper."

Helen was no expert on murder, but she felt certain that the Ripper hadn't boasted a hook. It seemed churlish to question the truth of Anne-Marie's story, however; though she silently wondered how much of this—the eyes taken out, the body rotting in the flat, the hook—was elaboration. The most scrupulous of reporters was surely tempted to embellish a story once in a while.

Anne-Marie had poured herself another cup of tea and was about to do the same for her guest.

"No thank you," Helen said. "I really should go."

"You married?" Anne-Marie asked, out of the blue.

"Yes. To a lecturer from the university."

"What's his name?"

"Trevor."

Anne-Marie put two heaped spoonfuls of sugar into her cup of tea. "Will you be coming back?" she asked.

"Yes, I hope to. Later in the week. I want to take some photographs of the pictures in the maisonette across the court."

"Well, call in."

"I shall. And thank you for your help."

"That's all right," Anne-Marie replied. "You've got to tell somebody, haven't you?"

•

"The man apparently had a hook instead of a hand."

Trevor looked up from his plate of *tagliatelle con prosciutto*. "Beg your pardon?"

Helen had been at pains to keep her recounting of this story as uncolored by her own response as she could. She was interested to know what Trevor would make of it, and she knew that if she once signaled her own stance he would instinctively take an opposing view out of plain bloody-mindedness.

"He had a hook," she repeated, without inflection.

Trevor put down his fork and plucked at his nose, sniffing. "I didn't read anything about this," he said.

"You don't read the local papers," Helen returned. "Neither of us do. Maybe it never made any of the nationals."

"'Geriatric Murdered by Hook-Handed Maniac'?" Trevor said, savoring the hyperbole. "I would have thought it very newsworthy. When was all of this supposed to have happened?"

"Sometime last summer. Maybe we were in Ireland."

"Maybe," said Trevor, taking up his fork again. Bending to his food, the polished lens of his spectacles reflected only the plate of pasta and chopped ham in front of him, not his eyes.

"Why do you say *maybe*?" Helen prodded.

"It doesn't sound quite right," he said. "In fact it sounds bloody preposterous."

"You don't believe it?" Helen said.

Trevor looked up from his food, tongue rescuing a speck of *tagliatelle* from the corner of his mouth. His face had relaxed into that noncommittal expression of his—the same face he wore, no doubt, when listening to his students. "Do *you* believe it?" he asked Helen. It was a favorite time-gaining device of his, another seminar trick, to question the questioner.

"I'm not certain," Helen replied, too concerned with finding some solid ground in this sea of doubts to waste energy scoring points.

"All right, forget the tale," Trevor said, deserting his food for another glass of red wine. "What about the teller? Did you trust her?"

Helen pictured Anne-Marie's earnest expression as she told the story of the old man's murder. "Yes," she said. "Yes, I think I would have known if she'd been lying to me."

"So why's it so important, anyhow? I mean, whether she's lying or not, what the fuck does it matter?"

It was a reasonable question, if irritatingly put. Why *did* it matter? Was it that she wanted to have her worst feelings about Spector Street proved false? That such an estate be filthy, be hopeless, be a dump where the undesirable and the disadvantaged were tucked out of public view—all that was a liberal commonplace, and she accepted it as an unpalatable social reality. But the story of the old man's murder and mutilation was something other. An image of violent death that, once with her, refused to part from her company.

She realized, to her chagrin, that this confusion was plain on her face, and that Trevor, watching her across the table, was not a little entertained by it.

"If it bothers you so much," he said, "why don't you go back there and ask around, instead of playing believe-it-or-not over dinner?"

She couldn't help but rise to his remark. "I thought you liked guessing games," she said.

He threw her a sullen look. "Wrong again," he said.

"No."

"Nothing at all? You don't remember anybody getting killed?"

"No," the boy said again, with impressive finality. "I don't remember."

"Well; thank you anyway."

This time, when she retraced her steps back to the car, the boy didn't follow. But as she turned the corner out of the quadrangle she glanced back to see him standing on the spot where she'd left him, staring after her as if she were a mad-woman.

By the time she had reached the car and packed the pho-tographic equipment into the trunk there were specks of rain in the wind, and she was sorely tempted to forget she'd ever heard Anne-Marie's story and make her way home, where the coffee would be warm even if the welcome wasn't. But she needed an answer to the question Trevor had put the previous night. Do *you* believe it? he'd asked when she'd told him the story. She hadn't known how to answer then, and she still didn't. Perhaps (why did she sense this?) the terminology of verifiable truth was redundant here; perhaps the final answer to his question was not an answer at all, only another question. If so, so. She had to find out.

Ruskin Court was as forlorn as its fellows, if not more so. It didn't even boast a bonfire. On the third floor balcony a woman was taking washing in before the rain broke; on the grass in the center of the quadrangle two dogs were absent-mindedly rutting, the fuckee staring up at the blank sky. As she walked along the empty pavement she set her face deter-minedly; a purposeful look, Bernadette had once said, deterred attack. When she caught sight of two women talking at the far end of the court she crossed over to them hurriedly, grateful for their presence.

"Excuse me?"

The women, both middle-aged, ceased their animated ex-change and looked her over.

"I wonder if you can help me?"

She could feel their appraisal, and their distrust; they went undisguised. One of the pair, her face florid, said plainly, "What do you want?"

Helen suddenly felt bereft of the least power to charm. What was she to say to these two that wouldn't make her motives appear ghoulish? "I was told . . . ," she began, and then stumbled, aware that she would get no assistance from either woman. ". . . I was told there'd been a murder near here. Is that right?"

The florid woman raised eyebrows so plucked they were barely visible. "Murder?" she said.

"Are you from the press?" the other woman inquired. The years had soured her features beyond sweetening. Her small mouth was deeply lined; her hair, which had been dyed brunette, showed a half-inch of gray at the roots.

"No, I'm not from the press," Helen said. "I'm a friend of Anne-Marie's, in Butts's Court." This claim of *friend* stretched the truth, but it seemed to mellow the women somewhat.

"Visiting, are you?" the florid woman asked.

"In a manner of speaking—"

"You missed the warm spell—"

"Anne-Marie was telling me about somebody who'd been murdered here, during the summer. I was curious about it."

"Is that right?"

"Do you know anything about it?"

"Lots of things go on around here," said the second woman. "You don't know the half of it."

"So it's true," Helen said.

"They had to close the toilets," the first woman put in.

"That's right. They did," the other said.

"The toilets?" Helen said. What had this to do with the old man's death?

"It was terrible," the first said. "Was it your Frank, Josie, who told you about it?"

"No, not Frank," Josie replied. "Frank was still at sea. It was Mrs. Tyzack."

The witness established, Josie relinquished the story to her companion, and turned her gaze back upon Helen. The suspicion had not yet died from her eyes.

"This was only the month before last," Josie said. "Just about the end of August. It was August, wasn't it?" She looked to the other woman for verification. "You've got the head for dates, Maureen."

Maureen looked uncomfortable. "I forget," she said, clearly unwilling to offer testimony.

"I'd like to know," Helen said. Josie, despite her companion's reluctance, was eager to oblige.

"There's some lavatories," she said, "outside the shops—you know, public lavatories. I'm not quite sure how it all happened exactly, but there used to be a boy . . . well, he wasn't a boy really. I mean he was a man of twenty or more, but he was"— she fished for the words—"mentally subnormal, I suppose you'd say. His mother used to have to take him around like he was a four-year-old. Anyhow, she let him go into the lavatories while she went to that little supermarket, what's it called?" She turned to Maureen for prompting, but the other woman just looked back, her disapproval plain. Josie was ungovernable, however. "Broad daylight, this was," she said to Helen. "Middle of the day. Anyhow, the boy went to the toilet, and the mother was in the shop. And after a while, you know how you do, she's busy shopping, she forgets about him, and then she thinks he's been gone a long time . . ."

At this juncture Maureen couldn't prevent herself from butting in: the accuracy of the story apparently took precedence over her wariness.

"She got into an argument," she corrected Josie, "with the manager. About some bad bacon she'd had from him. That was why she was such a time."

"I see," said Helen.

"Anyway," said Josie, picking up the tale, "she finished her shopping and when she came out he still wasn't there—"

"So she asked someone from the supermarket—" Maureen began, but Josie wasn't about to have her narrative snatched away at this vital juncture.

"She asked one of the men from the supermarket," she repeated over Maureen's interjection, "to go down into the lavatory and find him."

"It was terrible," said Maureen, clearly picturing the atrocity in her mind's eye.

"He was lying on the floor, in a pool of blood."

"Murdered?"

Josie shook her head. "He'd have been better off dead. He'd been attacked with a razor"—she let this piece of information sink in before delivering the *coup de grâce*,—"and they'd cut off his private parts. Just cut them off and flushed them down a toilet. No reason on earth to do it."

"Oh my God."

"Better off dead," Josie repeated. "I mean, they can't mend something like that, can they?"

The appalling tale was rendered worse still by the *sangfroid* of the teller, and by the casual repetition of "Better off dead."

"The boy," Helen said. "Was he able to describe his attackers?"

"No," said Josie, "he's practically an imbecile. He can't string more than two words together."

"And nobody saw anyone go into the lavatory? Or leaving it?"

"People come and go all the time," Maureen said. This, though it sounded like an adequate explanation, had not been Helen's experience. There was not a great bustle in the quadrangle and passageways; far from it. Perhaps the shopping mall was busier, she reasoned, and might offer adequate cover for such a crime.

"So they haven't found the culprit," she said.

"No," Josie replied, her eyes losing their fervor. The crime and its immediate consequences were the nub of this story; she had little or no interest in either the culprit or his capture.

"We're not safe in our own bed," Maureen observed. "You ask anyone."

"Anne-Marie said the same," Helen replied. "That's how she came to tell me about the old man. Said he was murdered during the summer, here in Ruskin Court."

"I do remember something," Josie said. "There *was* some talk I heard. An old man, and his dog. He was battered to death, and the dog ended up...I don't know. It certainly wasn't here. It must have been one of the other estates."

"Are you sure?"

The woman looked offended by this slur on her memory. "Oh yes," she said, "I mean if it had been here, we'd have known the story, wouldn't we?"

•

Helen thanked the pair for their help and decided to take a stroll around the quadrangle anyway, just to see how many more maisonettes were unoccupied. As in Butts's Court, many of the curtains were drawn and all the doors locked. But then if Spector Street *was* under siege from a maniac capable of the murder and mutilation such as she'd heard described, she was not surprised that the residents took to their homes and stayed there. There was nothing much to see around the court. All the unoccupied maisonettes and flats had been recently sealed, to judge by a litter of nails left on a doorstep by the council workmen. One sight *did* catch her attention however. Scrawled on the paving stones she was walking over—and all but erased by rain and the passage of feet—the same phrase she'd seen in the bedroom of number 14: "Sweets to the sweet." The words were so benign; why did she seem to sense menace in them? Was it in their excess, perhaps, in the sheer overabundance of sugar upon sugar, honey upon honey?

She walked on, though the rain persisted, away from the quadrangles and into a concrete no-man's-land through which she had not previously passed. This was—or had been—the site of the estate's amenities. Here was the children's playground, its metal-framed rides overturned, its sandpit fouled by dogs, its paddling pool empty. And here too were the shops. Several had been boarded up; those that hadn't were dingy and unattractive, their windows protected by heavy wire-mesh.

She walked along the row, and rounded a corner, and there in front of her was a squat brick building. The public lavatory, she guessed, though the signs designating it as such had gone. The iron gates were closed and padlocked. Standing in front of the charmless building, the wind gusting around her legs, she couldn't help but think of what had happened here. Of the man-child, bleeding on the floor, helpless to cry out. It made her queasy even to contemplate it. She turned her thoughts instead to the felon. What would he look like, she wondered, a man capable of such a depravity? She tried to make an image of him, but no detail she could conjure up carried sufficient force. But then monsters were seldom very terrible once hauled into the plain light of day. As long as this man was known only by his deeds he held untold power over the imagination; but the human truth beneath the terrors would, she knew, be bitterly disappointing. No monster he, just a whey-faced apology for a man more needful of pity than awe.

The next gust of wind brought the rain on more heavily. It was time, she decided, to be done with adventures for the day. Turning her back on the public lavatories, she hurried back through the quadrangles to the refuge of the car, the icy rain needling her face to numbness.

•

The dinner guests looked gratifyingly appalled at the story, and Trevor, to judge by the expression on his face, was furious.

It was done now, however; there was no taking it back. Nor could she deny the satisfaction she took in having silenced the interdepartmental babble about the table. It was Bernadette, Trevor's assistant in the history department, who broke the agonizing hush.

"When was this?"

"During the summer," Helen told her.

"I don't recall reading about it," said Archie, much the better for two hours of drinking; it mellowed a tongue that was otherwise fulsome in its self-coruscation.

"Perhaps the police are suppressing it," Daniel commented.

"Conspiracy?" said Trevor, plainly cynical.

"It's happening all the time," Daniel shot back.

"Why should they suppress something like this?" Helen said. "It doesn't make sense."

"Since when has police procedure made sense?" Daniel replied.

Bernadette cut in before Helen could answer. "We don't even bother to read about these things any longer," she said.

"Speak for yourself," somebody piped up, but she ignored them and went on:

"We're punch-drunk with violence. We don't see it any longer, even when it's in front of our noses."

"On the screen every night," Archie put in. "Death and disaster in full color."

"There's nothing very modern about that," Trevor said. "An Elizabethan would have seen death all the time. Public executions were a very popular form of entertainment."

The table broke up into a cacophony of opinions. After two hours of polite gossip the dinner party had suddenly caught fire. Listening to the debate rage, Helen was sorry she hadn't had time to have the photographs processed and printed; the graffiti would have added further fuel to this exhilarating row. It was Purcell, as usual, who was the last to weigh in with his point of view; and—again, as usual—it was devastating.

"Of course, Helen, my sweet," he began, that affected weariness in his voice edged with the anticipation of controversy, "your witnesses could all be lying, couldn't they?"

The talking around the table dwindled, and all heads turned in Purcell's direction. Perversely, he ignored the attention he'd garnered and turned to whisper in the ear of the boy he'd brought—a new passion who would, as in the past, be discarded in a matter of weeks for another pretty urchin.

"Lying?" Helen said. She could already feel herself bristling at the observation, and Purcell had spoken only a dozen words.

"Why not?" the other replied, lifting his glass of wine to his lips. "Perhaps they're all weaving some elaborate fiction or other. The story of the spastic's mutilation in the public toilet. The murder of the old man. Even that hook. All quite familiar elements. You must be aware that there's something *traditional* about these atrocity stories. One used to exchange them all the time; there was a certain *frisson* in them. Something competitive maybe, in attempting to find a new detail to add to the collective fiction; a fresh twist that would render the tale that little bit more appalling when you passed it on."

"It may be familiar to you—" Helen said defensively. Purcell was always so *poised*; it irritated her. Even if there were validity in his argument, which she doubted, she was damned if she'd concede it. "—I've never heard this kind of story before."

"Haven't you?" said Purcell, as though she were admitting to illiteracy. "What about the lovers and the escaped lunatic, have you heard that one?"

"I've heard that," Daniel said.

"The lover is disemboweled—usually by a hook-handed man—and the body left on the top of the car, while the fiancé cowers inside. It's a cautionary tale, warning of the evils of rampant heterosexuality." The joke won a round of laughter from everyone but Helen. "These stories are very common."

"So you're saying that they're telling me lies," she protested.

"Not lies, exactly—"

"You said *lies*."

"I was being provocative," Purcell returned, his placatory tone more enraging than ever. "I don't mean to imply there's any serious mischief in it. But you must concede that so far you haven't met a single *witness*. All these events have happened at some unspecified date to some unspecified person. They are reported at several removes. They occurred at best to the brothers of friends of distant relations. Please consider the possibility that perhaps these events do not exist in the real world at all, but are merely titillation for bored housewives."

Helen didn't make an argument in return, for the simple reason that she lacked one. Purcell's point about the conspicuous absence of witnesses was perfectly sound; she herself had wondered about it. It was strange, too, the way the women in Ruskin Court had speedily consigned the old man's murder to another estate, as though these atrocities always occurred just out of sight—around the next corner, down the next passageway—but never *here*.

"So why?" said Bernadette.

"Why what?" Archie puzzled.

"The stories. Why tell these horrible stories if they're not true?"

"Yes," said Helen, throwing the controversy back into Purcell's ample lap. "*Why?*"

Purcell preened himself, aware that his entry into the debate had changed the basic assumption at a stroke. "I don't know," he said, happy to be done with the game now that he'd shown his arm. "You really mustn't take me too seriously, Helen. *I* try not to." The boy at Purcell's side tittered.

"Maybe it's simply taboo material," Archie said.

"Suppressed—" Daniel prompted.

"Not the way you mean it," Archie retorted. "The whole world isn't politics, Daniel."

"Such naiveté."

"What's so taboo about death?" Trevor said. "Bernadette

already pointed out: it's in front of us all the time. Television, newspapers."

"Maybe that's not close enough," Bernadette suggested.

"Does anyone mind if I smoke?" Purcell broke in. "Dessert seems to have been indefinitely postponed."

Helen ignored the remark and asked Bernadette what she meant by "not close enough."

Bernadette shrugged. "I don't know precisely," she confessed, "maybe just that death has to be *near*; we have to *know* it's just around the corner. The television's not intimate enough."

Helen frowned. The observation made some sense to her, but in the clutter of the moment she couldn't root out its significance.

"Do you think they're stories too?" she asked.

"Andrew has a point—" Bernadette replied.

"Most kind," said Purcell. "Has somebody got a match? The boy's pawned my lighter."

"—about the absence of witnesses."

"All that proves is that I haven't met anybody who's actually *seen* anything," Helen encountered, "not that witnesses don't exist."

"All right," said Purcell. "Find me one. If you can prove to me that your atrocity monger actually lives and breathes, I'll stand everyone dinner at Apollinaire's. How's that? Am I generous to a fault, or do I just know when I can't lose?" He laughed, knocking on the table with his knuckles by way of applause.

"Sounds good to me," said Trevor. "What do you say, Helen?"

•

She didn't go back to Spector Street until the following Monday, but all weekend she was there in thought: standing outside the locked toilet, with the wind bringing rain; or in the bedroom, the portrait looming. Thoughts of the estate claimed all her concern. When, late on Saturday afternoon, Trevor found some petty reason for an argument, she let the insults pass, watching him perform the familiar ritual of self-martyrdom without being touched by it in the least. Her in-difference only enraged him further. He stormed out in high dudgeon, to visit whichever of his women was in favor this month. She was glad to see the back of him. When he failed to return that night she didn't even think of weeping about it. He was foolish and vacuous. She despaired of ever seeing a haunted look in his dull eyes; and what worth was a man who could not be haunted?

He did not return Sunday night either, and it crossed her mind the following morning, as she parked the car in the heart of the estate, that nobody even knew she had come, and that she might lose herself for days here and nobody would be any the wiser. Like the old man Anne-Marie had told her about: lying forgotten in his favorite armchair with his eyes hooked out, while the flies feasted and the butter went rancid on the table.

It was almost Bonfire Night, and over the weekend the small heap of combustibles in Butts's Court had grown to a sub-stantial size. The construction looked unsound, but that didn't prevent a number of boys from clambering over and into it. Much of its bulk was made up of furniture, filched, no doubt, from boarded-up properties. She doubted if it could burn for any time: if it did, it would be chokingly smoky. Four times, on her way across to Anne-Marie's house, she was waylaid by children begging for money to buy fireworks.

"Penny for the guy," they'd say, though none had a guy to display. She had emptied her pockets of change by the time she reached the front door.

Anne-Marie was in today, though there was no welcoming smile. She simply stared at her visitor as if mesmerized.

"I hope you don't mind me calling..."

Anne-Marie made no reply.

"... I just wanted a word."

"I'm busy," the woman finally announced. There was no invitation inside, no offer of tea.

"Oh. Well ... it won't take more than a moment."

The back door was open and a draft blew through the house. Papers were flying about in the backyard. Helen could see them lifting into the air like vast white moths.

"What do you want?" Anne-Marie asked.

"Just to ask you about the old man."

The woman frowned minutely. She looked as if she might be sick. Helen thought her face had the color and texture of stale dough. Her hair was lank and greasy.

"What old man?"

"Last time I was here, you told me about an old man who'd been murdered, do you remember?"

"No."

"You said he lived in the next court."

"I don't remember," Anne-Marie said.

"But you *distinctly* told me—"

Something fell to the floor in the kitchen and smashed. Anne-Marie flinched but did not move from the doorstep, her arm barring Helen's way into the house. The hallway was littered with the child's toys, gnawed and battered.

"Are you all right?"

Anne-Marie nodded. "I've got work to do," she said.

"And you don't remember telling me about the old man?"

"You must have misunderstood," Anne-Marie replied, and then, her voice hushed: "You shouldn't have come. Everybody *knows*."

"Knows what?"

The girl had begun to tremble. "You don't understand, do you? You think people aren't watching?"

"What does it matter? All I asked was—"

"I don't know *anything*," Anne-Marie reiterated. "Whatever I said to you, I lied about it."

"Well, thank you anyway," Helen said, too perplexed by the confusion of signals from Anne-Marie to press the point any further. Almost as soon as she had turned from the door she heard the lock snap closed behind her.

•

That conversation was only one of several disappointments that morning brought. Helen went back to the row of shops and visited the supermarket that Josie had spoken of. There she inquired about the lavatories and their recent history. The supermarket had changed hands only in the last month, and the new owner, a taciturn Pakistani, insisted that he knew nothing of when or why the lavatories had been closed. She was aware, as she made her inquiries, of being scrutinized by the other customers in the store; she felt like a pariah. That feeling deepened when, after leaving the supermarket, she saw Josie emerging from the launderette and called after her, only to have the woman pick up her pace and duck away into the maze of corridors. Helen followed but rapidly lost both her quarry and her way.

Frustrated to the verge of tears, she stood among the overturned rubbish bags and felt a surge of contempt for her foolishness. She didn't belong here, did she? How many times had she criticized others for their presumption in claiming to understand societies they had merely viewed from afar? And here was she, committing the same crime, coming here with her camera and her questions, using the lives (and deaths) of these people as fodder for party conversation. She didn't blame Anne-Marie for turning her back; had she deserved better?

Tired and chilled, she decided it was time to concede Purcell's point. It *was* all fiction she had been told. They had played with her—sensing her desire to be fed some horrors—

and she, the perfect fool, had fallen for every ridiculous word. It was time to pack up her credulity and go home.

One call demanded to be made before she returned to the car however: she wanted to look a final time at the painted head. Not as an anthropologist among an alien tribe, but as a confessed ghost train rider: for the thrill of it. Arriving at number 14, however, she faced the last and most crushing disappointment. The maisonette had been sealed up by conscientious council workmen. The door was locked; the front window boarded over.

She was determined not to be so easily defeated however. She made her way around the back of Butts's Court and located the yard of number 14 by simple mathematics. The gate was wedged closed from the inside, but she pushed hard against it, and with the effort, it opened. A heap of rubbish—rotted carpets, a box of rain-sodden magazines, a denuded Christmas tree—had blocked it.

She crossed the yard to the boarded-up windows and peered through the slats of wood. It wasn't bright outside, but it was darker still within; it was difficult to catch more than the vaguest hint of the painting on the bedroom wall. She pressed her face close to the wood, eager for a final glimpse.

A shadow moved across the room, momentarily blocking her view. She stepped back from the window, startled, not certain of what she'd seen. Perhaps merely her own shadow, cast through the window? But then *she* hadn't moved; it had.

She approached the window again, more cautiously. The air vibrated; she could hear a muted whine from somewhere, though she couldn't be certain whether it came from inside or out. Again, she put her face to the rough boards, and suddenly, something leaped at the window. This time she let out a cry. There was a scrabbling sound from within as nails raked the wood.

A dog! And a big one to have jumped so high.

"Stupid," she told herself aloud. A sudden sweat bathed her.

The scrabbling had stopped almost as soon as it had started, but she couldn't bring herself to go back to the window. Clearly the workmen who had sealed up the maisonette had failed to check it properly and incarcerated the animal by mistake. It was ravenous, to judge by the slavering she'd heard; she was grateful she hadn't attempted to break in. The dog—hungry, maybe half-mad in the stinking darkness—could have taken out her throat.

She stared at the boarded-up window. The slits between the boards were barely a half-inch wide, but she sensed that the animal was up on its hind legs on the other side, watching her through the gap. She could hear its panting now that her own breath was regularizing; she could hear its claws raking the sill.

"Bloody thing . . . ," she said. "Damn well stay in there."

She backed off toward the gate. Hosts of wood lice and spiders, disturbed from their nests by the moving of the carpets behind the gate, were scurrying underfoot, looking for a fresh darkness to call home.

She closed the gate behind her and was making her way around the front of the block when she heard the sirens; two ugly spirals of sound that made the hair on the back of her neck tingle. They were approaching. She picked up her speed, and came around into Butts's Court in time to see several policemen crossing the grass behind the bonfire and an ambulance mounting the pavement and driving around to the other side of the quadrangle. People had emerged from their flats and were standing on their balconies, staring down. Others were walking around the court, nakedly curious, to join a gathering congregation. Helen's stomach seemed to drop to her bowels when she realized *where* the hub of interest lay: at Anne-Marie's doorstep. The police were clearing a path through the throng for the ambulance men. A second police car had followed the route of the ambulance onto the pavement; two plainclothes officers were getting out.

She walked to the periphery of the crowd. What little talk

there was among the onlookers was conducted in low voices; one or two of the older women were crying. Though she peered over the heads of the spectators she could see nothing. Turning to a bearded man, whose child was perched on his shoulders, she asked what was going on. He didn't know. Somebody dead, he'd heard, but he wasn't certain.

"Anne-Marie?" she asked.

A woman in front of her turned and said: "You know her?" almost awed, as if speaking of a loved one.

"A little," Helen replied hesitantly. "Can you tell me what's happened?"

The woman involuntarily put her hand to her mouth, as if to stop the words before they came. But here they were nevertheless: "The child—" she said.

"Kerry?"

"Somebody got into the house around the back. Slit his throat."

Helen felt the sweat come again. In her mind's eye the newspapers rose and fell in Anne-Marie's yard.

"No," she said.

"Just like that."

She looked at the tragedienne who was trying to sell her this obscenity, and said "No" again. It defied belief; yet her denials could not silence the horrid comprehension she felt.

She turned her back on the woman and jostled her way out of the crowd. There would be nothing to see, she knew, and even if there had been she had no desire to look. These people—still emerging from their homes as the story spread—were exhibiting an appetite she was disgusted by. She was not one of them; would never *be* one of them. She wanted to slap every eager face into sense; wanted to say: "It's pain and grief you're going to spy on. Why? Why?" But she had no courage left. Revulsion had drained her of all but the energy to wander away, leaving the crowd to its sport.

Trevor had come home. He did not attempt an explanation of his absence but waited for her to cross-question him. When she failed to do so he sank into an easy *bonhomie* that was worse than his expectant silence. She was dimly aware that her lack of interest was probably more unsettling for him than the histrionics he had been anticipating. She couldn't have cared less.

She tuned the radio to the local station and listened for news. It came surely enough, confirming what the woman in the crowd had told her. Kerry Latimer was dead. Person or persons unknown had gained access to the house via the back-yard and murdered the child while he played on the kitchen floor. A police spokesman mouthed the usual platitudes, describing Kerry's death as an "unspeakable crime," and the miscreant as "a dangerous and deeply disturbed individual." For once, the rhetoric seemed justified, and the man's voice shook discernibly when he spoke of the scene that had confronted the officers in the kitchen of Anne-Marie's house.

"Why the radio?" Trevor casually inquired, when Helen had listened for news through three consecutive bulletins. She saw no point in withholding her experience at Spector Street from him; he would find out sooner or later. Coolly, she gave him a bald outline of what had happened at Butts's Court.

"This Anne-Marie is the woman you first met when you went to the estate. Am I right?"

She nodded, hoping he wouldn't ask her too many questions. Tears were close, and she had no intention of breaking down in front of him.

"So you were right," he said.

"Right?"

"About the place having a maniac."

"No," she said. "No."

"But the kid—"

She got up and stood at the window, looking down two stories into the darkened street below. Why did she feel the need to reject the conspiracy theory so urgently? Why was she now praying that Purcell had been right, and that all she'd been told had been lies? She went back to the way Anne-Marie had been when she'd visited her that morning: pale, jittery; *expectant*. She had been like a woman anticipating some arrival, hadn't she, eager to shoo unwanted visitors away so that she could turn back to the business of waiting? But waiting for what, or *whom?* Was it possible that Anne-Marie actually knew the murderer? Had perhaps invited him into the house?

"I hope they find the bastard," she said, still watching the street.

"They will," Trevor replied. "A baby murderer, for Christ's sake. They'll make it a high priority."

A man appeared at the corner of the street, turned, and whistled. A large Alsatian came to heel, and the two set off down toward the cathedral.

"The dog," Helen murmured.

"What?"

She had forgotten the dog in all that had followed. Now the shock she'd felt as it had leaped at the window shook her again.

"What dog?" Trevor pressed her.

"I went back to the flat today—where I took the pictures of the graffiti. There was a dog in there. Locked in."

"So?"

"It'll starve. Nobody knows it's there."

"How do you know it wasn't locked in to kennel it?"

"It was making such a noise," she said.

"Dogs bark," Trevor replied. "That's all they're good for."

"No," she said very quietly, remembering the noises through the boarded window. "It didn't bark."

"Forget the dog," Trevor said. "And the child. There's nothing you can do about it. You were just passing through."

His words only echoed her own thoughts of earlier in the day, but somehow, for reasons that she could find no words to convey, that conviction had decayed in the last hours. She was not just passing through. Nobody ever just *passed through*; experience always left its mark. Sometimes it merely scratched; on occasion it took off limbs. She did not know the extent of her present wounding, but she knew it was more profound than she yet understood, and it made her afraid.

"We're out of booze," she said, emptying the last dribble of whiskey into her tumbler.

Trevor seemed pleased to have a reason to be accommodating. "I'll go out, shall I?" he said. "Get a bottle or two?"

"Sure," she replied. "If you like."

He was gone only half an hour; she would have liked him to be longer. She didn't want to talk, only to sit and think through the unease in her belly. Though Trevor had dismissed her concern for the dog—and perhaps justifiably so—she couldn't help but go back to the locked maisonette in her mind's eye: to picture again the raging face on the bedroom wall, and hear the animal's muffled growl as it pawed the boards over the window. Whatever Trevor had said, she didn't believe the place was being used as a makeshift kennel. No, the dog was *imprisoned* in there, no doubt of it, running round and round, driven, in its desperation, to eat its own feces, growing more insane with every hour that passed. She became afraid that somebody—kids maybe, looking for more tinder for their bonfire—would break into the place, ignorant of what it contained. It wasn't that she feared for the intruders' safety, but that the dog, once liberated, would come for her. It would know where she was (so her drunken head construed) and come sniffing her out.

Trevor returned with the whiskey, and they drank together until the early hours, when her stomach revolted. She took refuge in the toilet—Trevor outside asking her if she needed anything, her telling him weakly to leave her alone. When,

an hour later, she emerged, he had gone to bed. She did not
join him but lay down on the sofa and dozed through until
dawn.

•

The murder was news. The next morning it made all the
tabloids as a front-page splash, and found prominent positions
in the heavyweights too. There were photographs of the stricken
mother being led from the house, and others, blurred but
potent, taken over the backyard wall and through the open
kitchen door. Was that blood on the floor, or shadow?

Helen did not bother to read the articles—her aching head
rebelled at the thought—but Trevor, who had brought the
newspapers in, was eager to talk. She couldn't work out if this
was further peacemaking on his part or a genuine interest in
the issue.

"The woman's in custody," he said, poring over the *Daily
Telegraph*. It was a paper he was politically averse to, but its
coverage of violent crime was notoriously detailed.

The observation demanded Helen's attention, unwilling or
not. "Custody?" she said. "Anne-Marie?"

"Yes."

"Let me see."

He relinquished the paper, and she glanced over the page.
"Third column," Trevor prompted.

She found the place, and there it was in black and white.
Anne-Marie had been taken into custody for questioning to
justify the time lapse between the estimated hour of the child's
death, and the time that it had been reported. Helen read the
relevant sentences over again, to be certain that she'd understood properly. Yes, she had. The police pathologist estimated
Kerry to have died between six and six-thirty that morning; the
murder had not been reported until twelve.

She read the report over a third and fourth time, but repetition did not change the horrid facts. The child had been

murdered before dawn. When she had gone to the house that
morning Kerry had already been dead four hours. The body
had been in the kitchen, a few yards down the hallway from
where she had stood, and Anne-Marie had said *nothing*. That
air of expectancy she had had about her—what had it signified?
That she awaited some cue to lift the receiver and call the
police?

"My Christ . . . ," Helen said, and let the paper drop.

"What?"

"I have to go to the police."

"Why?"

"To tell them I went to the house," she replied. Trevor
looked mystified. "The baby was dead, Trevor. When I saw
Anne-Marie yesterday morning, Kerry was already dead."

·

She rang the number given in the paper for any persons
offering information, and half an hour later a police car came
to pick her up. There was much that startled her in the two
hours of interrogation that followed, not least the fact that
nobody had reported her presence on the estate to the police,
though she had surely been noticed.

"They don't want to know," the detective told her. "You'd
think a place like that would be swarming with witnesses. If
it is, they're not coming forward. A crime like this—"

"Is it the first?" she said.

He looked at her across a chaotic desk. "First?"

"I was told some stories about the estate. Murders. This
summer."

The detective shook his head. "Not to my knowledge. There's
been a spate of muggings; one woman was put in hospital for
a week or so. But no; no murders."

She liked the detective. His eyes flattered her with their
lingering, and his face with its frankness. Past caring whether
she sounded foolish or not, she said: "Why do they tell lies

like that? About people having their eyes cut out. Terrible things."

The detective scratched his long nose. "We get it too," he said. "People come in here, they confess to all kinds of crap. Talk all night, some of them, about things they've done, or *think* they've done. Give you it all in the minutest detail. And when you make a few calls, it's all invented. Out of their minds."

"Maybe if they didn't tell you the stories . . . they'd actually go out and do it."

The detective nodded. "Yes," he said. "God help us. You might be right at that."

And the stories *she'd* been told, were they confessions of uncommitted crimes, accounts of the worst imaginable, imagined to keep fiction from becoming fact? The thought chased its own tail: these terrible stories still needed a *first cause*, a well-spring from which they leaped. As she walked home through the busy streets she wondered how many of her fellow citizens knew such stories. Were these inventions common currency, as Purcell had claimed? Was there a place, however small, reserved in every heart for the monstrous?

"Purcell rang," Trevor told her when she got home. "To invite us out to dinner."

The invitation wasn't welcome, and she made a face.

"Apollinaire's, remember?" he reminded her. "He said he'd take us all to dinner if you proved him wrong."

The thought of getting a dinner out of the death of Anne-Marie's infant was grotesque, and she said so.

"He'll be offended if you turn him down."

"I don't give a damn. I don't want dinner with Purcell."

"Please," he said softly. "He can get difficult, and I want to keep him smiling just at the moment."

She glanced across at him. The look he'd put on made him resemble a drenched spaniel. Manipulative bastard, she thought;

but said, "All right, I'll go. But don't expect any dancing on the tables."

"We'll leave that to Archie," he said. "I told Purcell we were free tomorrow night. Is that all right with you?"

"Whenever."

"He's booking a table for eight o'clock."

The evening papers had relegated The Tragedy of Baby Kerry to a few column inches on an inside page. In lieu of much fresh news they simply described the house-to-house inquiries that were now going on at Spector Street. Some of the later editions mentioned that Anne-Marie had been released from custody after an extended period of questioning and was now residing with friends. They also mentioned, in passing, that the funeral was to be the following day.

Helen had not entertained any thoughts of going back to Spector Street for the funeral when she went to bed that night, but sleep seemed to change her mind, and she woke with the decision made for her.

·

Death had brought the estate to life. Walking through to Ruskin Court from the street, she had never seen such numbers out and about. Many were already lining the curb to watch the funeral cortège pass, and looked to have claimed their niche early, despite the wind and the ever-present threat of rain. Some were wearing items of black clothing—a coat, a scarf— but the overall impression, despite the lowered voices and the studied frowns, was one of celebration. Children running around, untouched by reverence; occasional laughter escaping from between gossiping adults—Helen could feel an air of anticipation that made her spirits, despite the occasion, almost buoyant.

Nor was it simply the presence of so many people that reassured her; she was, she conceded to herself, happy to be back here in Spector Street. The quadrangles, with their stunted saplings and their gray grass, were more real to her than the carpeted corridors she was used to walking; the anonymous faces on the balconies and streets meant more than her colleagues at the university. In a word, she felt *home*.

Finally, the cars appeared, moving at a snail's pace through the narrow streets. As the hearse came into view—its tiny white casket decked with flowers—a number of women in the crowd gave quiet voice to their grief. One onlooker fainted; a knot of anxious people gathered around her. Even the children were stilled now.

Helen watched, dry-eyed. Tears did not come very easily to her, especially in company. As the second car, containing Anne-Marie and two other women, drew level with her, Helen saw that the bereaved mother was also eschewing any public display of grief. She seemed, indeed, to be almost elevated by the proceedings, sitting upright in the back of the car, her pallid features the source of much admiration. It was a sour thought, but Helen felt as though she was seeing Anne-Marie's finest hour; the one day in an otherwise anonymous life in which she was the center of attention. Slowly, the cortège passed by and disappeared from view.

The crowd around Helen was already dispersing. She detached herself from the few mourners who still lingered at the curb and wandered through from the street into Butts's Court. It was her intention to go back to the locked maisonette, to see if the dog was still there. If it was, she would put her mind at rest by finding one of the estate caretakers and informing him of the fact.

The quadrangle was, unlike the other courts, practically empty. Perhaps the residents, being neighbors of Anne-Marie's, had gone on to the crematorium for the service. Whatever the reason, the place was eerily deserted. Only children remained, playing around the pyramid bonfire, their voices echoing across the empty expanse of the square.

She reached the maisonette and was surprised to find the door open again, as it had been the first time she'd come here. The sight of the interior made her light-headed. How often in the past several days had she imagined standing here, gazing into that darkness. There was no sound from inside. The dog had surely run off—either that, or died. There could be no harm, could there, in stepping into the place one final time, just to look at the face on the wall, and its attendant slogan?

"Sweets to the sweet." She had never looked up the origins of that phrase. No matter, she thought. Whatever it had stood for once, it was transformed here, as everything was; herself included. She stood in the front room for a few moments, to allow herself time to savor the confrontation ahead. Far away behind her the children were screeching like mad birds.

She stepped over a clutter of furniture and toward the short corridor that joined living room to bedroom, still delaying the moment. Her heart was quick in her: a smile played on her lips.

And there! At last! The portrait loomed, compelling as ever. She stepped back in the murky room to admire it more fully and her heel caught on the mattress that still lay in the corner. She glanced down. The squalid bedding had been turned over, to present its untorn face. Some blankets and a rag-wrapped pillow had been tossed over it. Something glistened among the folds of the uppermost blanket. She bent down to look more closely and found there a handful of sweets—chocolates and caramels—wrapped in bright paper. And littered among them, neither so attractive nor so sweet, a dozen razor-blades. There was blood on several. She stood up again and backed away from the mattress, and as she did so a buzzing sound reached her ears from the next room. She turned, and the light in the bedroom diminished as a figure stepped into the gullet between her and the outside world. Silhouetted against the light, she could scarcely see the man in the doorway, but she smelled him. He smelled like cotton candy, and the buzzing was with him or in him.

"I just came to look," she said, "... at the picture."

The buzzing went on—the sound of a sleepy afternoon, far from here. The man in the doorway did not move.

"Well," she said, "I've seen what I wanted to see." She hoped against hope that her words would prompt him to stand aside and let her past, but he didn't move, and she couldn't find the courage to challenge him by stepping toward the door.

"I have to go," she said, knowing that despite her best efforts fear seeped between every syllable. "I'm expected..."

That was not entirely untrue. Tonight they were all invited to Apollinaire's for dinner. But that wasn't until eight, which was four hours away. She would not be missed for a long while yet.

"If you'll excuse me," she said.

The buzzing had quieted a little, and in the hush the man in the doorway spoke. His unaccented voice was almost as sweet as his scent.

"No need to leave yet," he breathed.

"I'm due...due..."

Though she couldn't see his eyes, she felt them on her, and they made her feel drowsy, like that summer that sang in her head.

"I came for you," he said.

She repeated the four words in her head. *I came for you*. If they were meant as a threat, they certainly weren't spoken as one.

"I don't...know you," she said.

"No," the man murmured. "But you doubted me."

"Doubted?"

"You weren't content with the stories, with what they wrote on the walls. So I was obliged to come."

The drowsiness slowed her mind to a crawl, but she grasped

the essentials of what the man was saying. That he was legend, and she, in disbelieving him, had obliged him to show his hand. She looked, now, down at those hands. One of them was missing. In its place, a hook.

"There will be some blame," he told her. "They will say your doubts shed innocent blood. But I say what's blood for, if not for shedding? And in time the scrutiny will pass. The police will leave, the cameras will be pointed at some fresh horror, and they will be left alone, to tell stories of the Candyman again."

"Candyman?" she said. Her tongue could barely shape that blameless word.

"I came for you," he murmured so softly that seduction might have been in the air. And so saying, he moved through the passageway and into the light.

She knew him, without doubt. She had known him all along, in that place kept for terrors. It was the man on the wall. His portrait painter had not been a fantasist: the picture that howled over her was matched in each extraordinary particular by the man she now set eyes upon. He was bright to the point of gaudiness: his flesh a waxy yellow, his thin lips pale blue, his wild eyes glittering as if their irises were set with rubies. His jacket was a patchwork, his trousers the same. He looked, she thought, almost ridiculous, with his blood-stained motley, and the hint of rouge on his jaundiced cheeks. But people were facile. They needed these shows and shams to keep their interest. Miracles; murders; demons driven out and stones rolled from tombs. The cheap glamour did not taint the sense beneath. It was only, in the natural history of the mind, the bright feathers that drew the species to mate with its secret self.

And she was almost enchanted. By his voice, by his colors, by the buzz from his body. She fought to resist the rapture; though. There was a *monster* here, beneath this fetching display; its nest of razors was at her feet, still drenched in blood. Would it hesitate to slit her own throat if it once laid hands on her?

As the Candyman reached for her she dropped down and snatched the blanket up, flinging it at him. A rain of razors and candy fell around his shoulders. The blanket followed, blinding him. But before she could snatch the moment to slip past him, the pillow that had lain on the blanket rolled in front of her.

It was not a pillow at all. Whatever the forlorn white casket she had seen in the hearse had contained, it was not the body of Baby Kerry. That was *here*, at her feet, its blood-drained face turned up to her. He was naked. His body showed everywhere signs of the fiend's attentions.

In the two heartbeats she took to register this last horror, the Candyman threw off the blanket. In his struggle to escape from its folds, his jacket had come unbuttoned, and she saw— though her senses protested—that the contents of his torso had rotted away, and the hollow was now occupied by a nest of bees. They swarmed in the vault of his chest, and encrusted in a seething mass the remnants of flesh that hung there. He smiled at her plain repugnance.

"Sweets to the sweet," he murmured, and stretched his hooked hand toward her face. She could no longer see light from the outside world or hear the children playing in Butts's Court. There was no escape into a saner world than this. The Candyman filled her sight; her drained limbs had no strength to hold him at bay.

"Don't kill me," she breathed.

"Do you believe in me?" he said.

She nodded minutely. "How can I not?" she said.

"Then why do you want to live?"

She didn't understand, and was afraid her ignorance would prove fatal, so she said nothing.

"If you would learn," the fiend said, "just a *little* from me
... you would not beg to live." His voice had dropped to a
whisper. "I am rumor," he sang in her ear. "It's a blessed
condition, believe me. To live in people's dreams; to be whispered at street corners, but not have to *be*. Do you understand?"

Her weary body understood. Her nerves, tired of jangling,
understood. The sweetness he offered was life without living:
was to be dead, but remembered everywhere; immortal in
gossip and graffiti.

"Be my victim," he said.

"No..." she murmured.

"I won't force it upon you," he replied, the perfect gentle-
man. "I won't oblige you to die. But think; *think*. If I kill you
here—if I unhook you"—he traced the path of the promised
wound with his hook; it ran from groin to neck—"think how
they would mark this place with their talk... point it out as
they passed by and say, '*She* died there, the woman with the
green eyes.' Your death would be a parable to frighten children
with. Lovers would use it as an excuse to cling closer together."

She had been right: this *was* a seduction.

"Was fame ever so easy?" he asked.

She shook her head. "I'd prefer to be forgotten," she replied,
"than be remembered like that."

He made a tiny shrug. "What do the good know?" he said.
"Except what the bad teach them by their excesses?" He raised
his hooked hand. "I said I would not oblige you to die and
I'm true to my word. Allow me, though, a kiss at least...."

He moved toward her. She murmured some nonsensical
threat, which he ignored. The buzzing in his body had risen
in volume. The thought of touching his body, of the proximity
of the insects, was horrid. She forced her lead-heavy arms up
to keep him at bay.

His lurid face eclipsed the portrait on the wall. She couldn't
bring herself to touch him, and instead stepped back. The

sound of the bees rose; some, in their excitement, had crawled up his throat and were flying from his mouth. They climbed about his lips; in his hair.

She begged him over and over to leave her alone, but he would not be placated. At last she had nowhere left to retreat to; the wall was at her back. Steeling herself against the stings, she put her hands on his crawling chest and pushed. As she did so his hand shot out and around the back of her neck, the hook nicking the flushed skin of her throat. She felt blood come; felt certain he would open her jugular in one terrible slash. But he had given his word, and he was true to it.

Aroused by this sudden activity, the bees were everywhere. She felt them moving on her, searching for morsels of wax in her ears, and sugar at her lips. She made no attempt to swat them away. The hook was at her neck. If she so much as moved it would wound her. She was trapped, as in her child-hood nightmares, with every chance of escape stymied. When sleep had brought her to such hopelessness—the demons on every side, waiting to tear her limb from limb—one trick re-mained. To let go; to give up all ambition to life, and leave her body to the dark. Now, as the Candyman's face pressed to hers, and the sound of bees blotted out even her own breath, she played that hidden hand. And, as surely as in dreams, the room and the fiend were painted out and gone.

•

She woke from brightness into dark. There were several panicked moments when she couldn't think of where she was, then several more when she remembered. But there was no pain about her body. She put her hand to her neck; it was, barring the nick of the hook, untouched. She was lying on the mattress she realized. Had she been assaulted as she lay in a faint? Gingerly, she investigated her body. She was not bleeding; her clothes were not disturbed. The Candyman had, it seemed, simply claimed his kiss.

She sat up. There was precious little light through the boarded window—and none from the front door. Perhaps it was closed, she reasoned. But no; even now she heard somebody whispering on the threshold. A woman's voice.

She didn't move. They were crazy, these people. They had known all along what her presence in Butts's Court had summoned, and they had *protected* him—this honeyed psychopath; given him a bed and an offering of bonbons, hidden him away from prying eyes, and kept their silence when he brought blood to their doorsteps. Even Anne-Marie, dry-eyed in the hallway of her house, knowing that her child was dead a few yards away.

The child! That was the evidence she needed. Somehow they had conspired to get the body from the casket (what had they substituted; a dead dog?) and brought it here to the Candyman's tabernacle as a toy, or a lover. She would take Baby Kerry with her—to the police—and tell the whole story. Whatever they believed of it, and that would probably be very little, the fact of the child's body was incontestable. That way at least some of the crazies would suffer for their conspiracy. Suffer for *her* suffering.

The whispering at the door had stopped. Now somebody was moving toward the bedroom. Whoever it was hadn't brought a light. Helen made herself small, hoping she might escape detection.

A figure appeared in the doorway. The gloom was too impenetrable for her to make out more than a slim figure, who bent down and picked up a bundle on the floor. A fall of blond hair identified the newcomer as Anne-Marie: the bundle she was picking up was undoubtedly Kerry's corpse. Without looking in Helen's direction, the mother about-faced and made her way out of the bedroom.

Helen listened as the footsteps receded across the living room. Swiftly, she got to her feet and crossed to the passageway. From there she could vaguely see Anne-Marie's outline in the doorway of the maisonette. No lights burned in the quadrangle beyond. The woman disappeared, and Helen followed as speedily as she could, eyes fixed on the door ahead. She stumbled once, and once again, but reached the door in time to see Anne-Marie's vague form in the night ahead.

She stepped out of the maisonette and into the open air. It was chilly; there were no stars. All the lights on the balconies and corridors were out, nor did any burn in the flats; not even the glow of a television. Butts's Court was deserted.

She hesitated before going in pursuit of the girl. Why didn't she slip away now, cowardice coaxed her, and find her way back to the car? But if she did that the conspirators would have time to conceal the child's body. When she got back here with the police there would be sealed lips and shrugs and she would be told she had imagined the corpse and the Candyman. All the terrors she had tasted would recede into rumor again. Into words on a wall. And every day she lived from now on she would loathe herself for not going in pursuit of sanity.

She followed. Anne-Marie was not making her way around the quadrangle but moving toward the center of the lawn in the middle of the court. To the bonfire! Yes; to the bonfire! It loomed in front of Helen now, blacker than the night sky. She could just make out Anne-Marie's figure, moving to the edge of the piled timbers and furniture, and ducking to climb into its heart. This was how they planned to remove the evidence. To bury the child was not certain enough; but to cremate it, and pulverize the bones—who would ever know?

She stood a dozen yards from the pyramid and watched as Anne-Marie climbed out again and moved away, folding her figure into the darkness.

Quickly, Helen moved through the long grass and located the narrow space in among the piled timbers into which Anne-Marie had put the body. She thought she could see the pale form; it had been laid in a hollow. She couldn't reach it however. Thanking God that she was as slim as the mother, she squeezed through the narrow aperture. Her dress snagged on a nail as she did so. She turned round to disengage it, fingers trembling. When she turned back she had lost sight of the corpse.

She fumbled blindly ahead of her, her hands finding wood and rags and what felt like the back of an old armchair, but not the cold skin of the child. She had hardened herself against contact with the body; she had endured worse in the last hours than picking up a dead baby. Determined not to be defeated, she advanced a little farther, her shins scraped and her fingers spiked with splinters. Flashes of light were appearing at the corners of her aching eyes; her blood whined in her ears. But there, *there!*—the body was no more than a yard and a half ahead of her. She ducked down to reach beneath a beam of wood, but her fingers missed the forlorn bundle by inches. She stretched farther, the whine in her head increasing, but still she could not reach the child. All she could do was bend double and squeeze into the hidey-hole the children had left in the center of the bonfire.

It was difficult to get through. The space was so small she could barely crawl on hands and knees, but she made it. The child lay facedown. She fought back the remnants of squeamishness and went to pick it up. As she did so, something landed on her arm. The shock startled her. She almost cried out, but swallowed the urge, and brushed the irritation away. It buzzed as it rose from her skin. The whine she had heard in her ears was not her blood but the hive.

"I knew you'd come," the voice behind her said, and a wide hand covered her face. She fell backward and the Candyman embraced her.

"We have to go," he said in her ear, as flickering light spilled between the stacked timbers. "Be on our way, you and I."

She fought to be free of him, to cry out for them not to light the bonfire, but he held her lovingly close. The light grew: warmth came with it; and through the kindling and the first flames she could see figures approaching the pyre out of the darkness of Butts's Court. They had been there all along: waiting, the lights turned out in their homes, and broken all along the corridors. Their final conspiracy.

The bonfire caught with a will, but by some trick of its construction the flames did not invade her hiding place quickly; nor did the smoke creep through the furniture to choke her. She was able to watch how the children's faces gleamed; how the parents called them from going too close, and how they disobeyed; how the old women, their blood thin, warmed their hands and smiled into the flames. Presently the roar and the crackle became deafening, and the Candyman let her scream herself hoarse in the certain knowledge that nobody could hear her, and even if they had, would not have moved to claim her from the fire.

The bees vacated the fiend's belly as the air became hotter, and mazed the air with their panicked flight. Some, attempting escape, caught fire, and fell like tiny meteors to the ground. The body of Baby Kerry, which lay close to the creeping flames, began to cook. Its downy hair smoked; its back blistered.

Soon the heat crept down Helen's throat and scorched her pleas away. She sank back, exhausted, into the Candyman's arms, resigned to his triumph. In moments they would be on their way, as he had promised, and there was no help for it.

Perhaps they would remember her, as he had said they might, finding her cracked skull in tomorrow's ashes. Perhaps she might become, in time, a story with which to frighten children. She had lied, saying she preferred death to such questionable fame. She did not. As to her seducer, he laughed as the conflagration sniffed them out. There was no permanence for him in this night's death. His deeds were on a hundred walls and ten thousand lips, and should he be doubted again his congregation could summon him with sweetness. He had reason to laugh. So, as the flames crept upon them, did she, as through the fire she caught sight of a familiar face moving between the onlookers. It was Trevor. He had forsaken his meal at Apollinaire's and come looking for her.

She watched him questioning this fire watcher and that, but they shook their heads, all the while staring at the pyre with smiles buried in their eyes. Poor dupe, she thought, following his antics. She willed him to look past the flames in the hope that he might see her burning. Not so that he could save her from death—she was long past hope of that—but because she pitied him in his bewilderment and wanted to give him, though he would not have thanked her for it, something to be haunted by. That, and a story to tell.

THE

MADONNA

JERRY COLOQHOUN WAITED ON THE STEPS OF THE LEOPOLD Road Swimming Pools for over thirty-five minutes before Garvey turned up. His feet were steadily losing feeling as the cold crept up through the soles of his shoes. The time would come, he reassured himself, when *he'd* be the one to keep people waiting. Indeed, such a prerogative might not be so far away, if he could persuade Ezra Garvey to invest in the Pleasure Dome. It would require an appetite for risk, and substantial assets, but his contacts had assured him that Garvey, whatever his reputation, possessed both in abundance. The source of the man's money was not an issue in the proceedings, or so Jerry had persuaded himself. Many a nicer plutocrat had turned the project down flat in the last six months; in such circumstances fineness of feeling was a luxury he could scarcely afford.

He was not all that surprised by the reluctance of investors. These were difficult times, and risks were not to be undertaken lightly. More, it took a measure of imagination, a faculty not overabundant among the moneyed he'd met, to see the Pools transformed into the gleaming amenity complex he envisaged. But his researches had convinced him that in an area like this—where houses once teetering on demolition were being bought up and refurbished by a generation of middle-class sybarites—that in such an area the facilities he had planned would scarcely fail to make money.

There was a further inducement. The Council, which owned the Pools, was eager to unload the property as speedily as possible; it had debtors aplenty. Jerry's bribee at the Directorate of Community Services—the same man who'd happily filched the keys to the property for two bottles of gin—had told him that the building could be purchased for a song if the offer was made swiftly. It was all a question of good timing.

A skill, apparently, that Garvey lacked. By the time he arrived the numbness had spread north to Jerry's knees, and his temper had worn thin. He made no show of it, however, as Garvey got out of his chauffeur-driven Rover and came up the steps. Jerry had only spoken to him by telephone and had expected a larger man, but despite the lack of stature there was no doubting Garvey's authority. It was there in the plain look of appraisal he gave Coloqhoun; in the joyless features; in the immaculate suit.

The pair shook hands.

"It's good to see you, Mr. Garvey."

The man nodded but returned no pleasantry. Jerry, eager to be out of the cold, opened the front door and led the way inside.

"I've only got ten minutes," Garvey said.

"Fine," Jerry replied. "I just wanted to show you the layout."

"You've surveyed the place?"

"Of course."

This was a lie. Jerry had been over the building the previous August, courtesy of a contact in the Architects' Department, and had, since that time, looked at the place from the outside several times. But it had been five months since he'd actually stepped into the building; he hoped accelerating decay had not taken an unshakable hold since then. They stepped into the vestibule. It smelled damp but not overpoweringly so.

"There's no electricity on," he explained. "We have to go by flashlight." He fished the heavy-duty flashlight from his pocket and trained the beam on the inner door. It was padlocked. He stared at the lock, dumbfounded. If this door had been locked last time he was here, he didn't remember. He tried the single key he'd been given, knowing before he put it to the lock that the two were hopelessly mismatched. He cursed under his breath, quickly skipping through the options available. Either he and Garvey about-faced, and left the Pools to its secrets—if mildew, creeping rot and a roof that was within an ace of surrender could be classed as secrets—or else he made an attempt to break in. He glanced at Garvey, who had taken a prodigious cigar from his inside pocket and was stroking the end with a flame; velvet smoke billowed.

"I'm sorry about the delay," he said.

"It happens," Garvey returned, clearly unperturbed.

"I think strong-arm tactics may be called for," Jerry said, feeling out the other man's response to a break-in.

"Suits me."

Jerry quickly rooted about the darkened vestibule for an implement. In the ticket booth he found a metal-legged stool. He hoisted it out of the booth and crossed back to the door, aware of Garvey's amused but benign gaze upon him, and, using one of the legs as a lever, broke the shackle of the padlock. The lock clattered to the tiled floor.

"Open sesame," he murmured with some satisfaction, and pushed the door open for Garvey.

The sound of the falling lock seemed still to linger in the deserted corridors when they stepped through, its din receding toward a sigh as it diminished. The interior looked more inhospitable than Jerry had remembered. The fitful daylight that fell through the mildewed panes of the skylights along the corridor was blue-gray—the light and that which it fell upon vying in dreariness. Once, no doubt, the Leopold Road Pools had been a showcase of Deco design—of shining tiles and cunning mosaics worked into floor and wall. But not in Jerry's adult life, certainly. The tiles underfoot had long since lifted with the damp; along the walls they had fallen in the hundreds, leaving patterns of white ceramic and dark plaster like some vast and clueless crossword puzzle. The air of destitution was so profound that Jerry had half a mind to give up his attempt at selling the project to Garvey on the spot. Surely there was no hope of a sale here, even at the ludicrously low asking price. But Garvey seemed more engaged than Jerry had allowed. He

was already stalking down the corridor, puffing on his cigar
and grunting to himself as he went. It could be no more than
morbid curiosity, Jerry felt, that took the developer deeper into
this echoing mausoleum. And yet:

"It's atmospheric. The place has possibilities," Garvey said.
"I don't have much of a reputation as a philanthropist, Coloqhoun—you must know that—but I've got a taste for some
of the finer things." He had paused in front of a mosaic de-
picting a nondescript mythological scene—fish, nymphs and
sea-gods at play. He grunted appreciatively, describing the
sinuous line of the design with the wet end of his cigar.

"You don't see craftsmanship like that nowadays," he commented.

Jerry thought it unremarkable but said, "It's superb."

"Show me the rest."

The complex had once boasted a host of facilities—sauna
rooms, Turkish baths, thermal baths—in addition to the two
pools. These various areas were connected by a warren of
passageways that, unlike the main corridor, had no skylights:
the flashlight had to suffice here. Dark or no, Garvey wanted
to see all the public areas. The ten minutes he had warned
were his limit stretched into twenty and thirty, the exploration
constantly brought to a halt as he discovered some new felicity
to comment upon. Jerry listened with feigned comprehension:
he found the man's enthusiasm for the decor confounding.

"I'd like to see the pools now," Garvey announced when
they'd made a thorough investigation of the subordinate amenities. Dutifully, Jerry led the way through the labyrinth toward
the two pools. In a small corridor a little way from the Turkish
baths Garvey said:

"Hush."

Jerry stopped walking. "What?"

"I heard a voice."

Jerry listened. The flashlight's beam, splashing off the tiles, threw a pale luminescence around them, which drained the blood from Garvey's features.

"I don't hear—"

"I said *hush*," Garvey snapped. He moved his head to and fro slowly. Jerry could hear nothing. Neither, now, could Garvey. He shrugged and pulled on his cigar. It had gone out, killed by the damp air.

"A trick of the corridors," Jerry said. "The echoes in the place are misleading. Sometimes you hear your own footsteps coming back to meet you."

Garvey grunted again. The grunt seemed to be his most valued part of speech. "I did hear something," he said, clearly not satisfied with Jerry's explanation. He listened again. The corridors were pin-drop hushed. It was not even possible to hear the traffic on Leopold Road. At last, Garvey seemed content.

"Lead on," he said. Jerry did just that, though the route to the pools was by no means clear to him. They took several wrong turnings, winding their way through a maze of identical corridors, before they reached their intended destination.

"It's warm," said Garvey as they stood outside the smaller of the two pools.

Jerry murmured his agreement. In his eagerness to reach the pools he had not noticed the steadily escalating temperature. But now that he stood still he could feel a film of sweat on his body. The air was humid, but it smelled not of damp and mildew, as elsewhere in the building. This was a sicklier, almost opulent, scent. He hoped Garvey, cocooned in the smoke of his relit cigar, could not share the smell; it was far from pleasant.

"The heating's on," Garvey said.

"It certainly seems like it," Jerry returned, though he couldn't think why. Perhaps the Department of Engineers warmed the heating system through once in a while, to keep it in working order. In which case, were they in the bowels of the building somewhere? Perhaps Garvey *had* heard voices? He mentally constructed a line of explanation should their paths cross.

"The pools," he said, and pulled open one of the double-doors. The skylight here was even dirtier than those in the main corridor; precious little light illuminated the scene. Garvey was not to be thwarted, however. He stepped through the door and across to the lip of the pool. There was little to see; the surfaces here were covered with several years' growth of mold. On the bottom of the pool, barely discernible beneath the algae, a design had been worked into the tiles. A bright fish-eye glanced up at them, perfectly thoughtless.

"Always had a fear of water," Garvey said ruminatively as he stared into the drained pool. "Don't know where it comes from."

"Childhood," Jerry ventured.

"I don't think so," the other replied. "My wife says it's the womb."

"The womb?"

"I didn't like swimming around in there, she says," he replied, with a smile that might have been at his own expense but was more likely at that of his wife.

A short sound came to meet them across the empty expanse of the pool, as of something falling. Garvey froze. "You hear *that*?" he said. "There's somebody in here." His voice had suddenly risen half an octave.

"Rats," Jerry replied. He wished to avoid an encounter with the engineers if possible; difficult questions might well be asked.

"Give me the torch," Garvey said, snatching it from Jerry's hand. He scanned the opposite side of the pool with the beam. It lit a series of dressing rooms, and an open door that led out of the pool. Nothing moved.

"I don't like vermin—" Garvey said.

"The place has been neglected," Jerry replied.

"—Especially the human variety." Garvey thrust the flash-

light back into Jerry's hands. "I've got enemies, Mr. Coloqhoun. But then you've done your research on me, haven't
you? You know I'm no lily-white." Garvey's concern about
the noises he thought he'd heard now made unpalatable sense.
It wasn't rats he was afraid of but grievous bodily harm. "I
think I should be going," he said. "Show me the other pool
and we'll be away."

"Surely." Jerry was as happy to be going as his guest. The
incident had raised his temperature. The sweat came profusely
now, trickling down the back of his neck. His sinuses ached.
He led Garvey across the hallway to the door of the larger pool
and pulled. The door refused him.

"Problem?"

"It must be locked from the inside."

"Is there another way in?"

"I think so. Do you want me to go round the back?"

Garvey glanced at his watch. "Two minutes," he said. "I've
got appointments."

Garvey watched Coloqhoun disappear down the darkened
corridor, the flashlight's beam running on ahead of him. He
didn't like the man. He was too closely shaven; and his shoes
were Italian. But—the proposer aside—the project had some
merit. Garvey liked the Pools with its adjuncts, the uniformity
of the design, the banality of the decorations. Unlike many,
he found institutions reassuring: hospitals, schools, even prisons. They smacked of social order; they soothed that part of
him fearful of chaos. Better a world too organized than one
not organized enough.

Again his cigar had gone out. He put it between his teeth
and lit a match. As the first flare died, he caught an inkling
sight of a naked girl in the corridor ahead, watching him. The
glimpse was momentary, but when the match dropped from
his fingers and the light failed, she appeared in his mind's eye,
perfectly remembered. She was young—fifteen at the most—
and her body full. The sweat on her skin lent her such sen-

suality she might have stepped from his dream-life. Dropping
his stale cigar, he rummaged for another match and struck it,
but in the meager seconds of darkness the child-beauty had
gone, leaving only the trace of her sweet body scent on the
air.

"Girl?" he said.

The sight of her nudity, and the shock in her eyes, made
him eager for her.

"Girl?"

The flame of the second match failed to penetrate more
than a yard or two down the corridor.

"Are you there?"

She could not be far, he reasoned. Lighting a third match,
he went in search of her. He had gone only a few steps when
he heard somebody behind him. He turned. The flashlight lit
the fright on his face. It was only the Italian Shoes.

"There's no way in."

"There's no need to blind me," Garvey said. The beam
dropped.

"I'm sorry."

"There's somebody here, Coloqhoun. A girl."

"A girl?"

"You know something about it maybe?"

"No."

"She was stark naked. Standing three or four yards from
me."

Jerry looked at Garvey, mystified. Was the man suffering
from sexual delusions?

"I tell you I saw a girl," Garvey protested, though no word
of contradiction had been offered. "If you hadn't arrived I'd
have had my hands on her." He glanced back down the corridor. "Get some light down there." Jerry trained the beam on
the maze. There was no sign of life.

"Damn," said Garvey, his regret quite genuine. He looked

back at Jerry. "All right," he said. "Let's get the hell out of here."

"I'm interested," he said, as they parted on the step. "The project has potential. Do you have a ground plan of the place?"

"No, but I can get my hands on one."

"Do that." Garvey was lighting a fresh cigar. "And send me your proposals in more detail. Then we'll talk again."

•

It took a considerable bribe to get the plans of the Pools out of his contact at the Architects' Department, but Jerry eventually secured them. On paper the complex looked like a labyrinth. And like the best labyrinths, there was no order apparent in the layout of shower rooms and bathrooms and changing rooms. It was Carole who proved that thesis to be wrong.

"What is this?" she asked him as he pored over the plans that evening. They'd had four or five hours together at his flat—hours without the bickering and the bad feeling that had soured their time together of late.

"It's the ground plan of the swimming pools on Leopold Road. Do you want another brandy?"

"No thanks." She peered at the plan while he got up to refill his glass.

"I think I've got Garvey in on the deal."

"You're going to do business with him, are you?"

"Don't make me sound like a white slaver. The man's got money."

"Dirty money."

"What's a little dirt between friends?"

She looked at him frostily, and he wished he could have played back the previous ten seconds and erased the comment.

"I *need* this project," he said, taking his drink across to the sofa and sitting opposite her, the ground plan spread on the low table between them. "I need something to go right for me for once."

Her eyes refused to grant him a reprieve.

"I just think Garvey and his like are bad news," she said. "I don't care how much money he's got. He's a villain, Jerry."

"So I should give the whole thing up, should I? Is that what you're saying?" They'd had this argument, in one guise or another, several times in the last few weeks. "I should just forget all the hard labor I've put in and add this failure to all the others?"

"There's no need to shout."

"I'm not shouting!"

She shrugged. "All right," she said quietly, "you're not shouting."

"Christ!"

She went back to perusing the ground plan. He watched her from over the rim of his whiskey tumbler; saw the parting down the middle of her head, and the fine blond hair that divided from there. They made so little sense to each other, he thought. The processes that brought them to their present impasse were perfectly obvious; yet time and again they failed to find the common ground necessary for a fruitful exchange of views. Not simply on this matter, on half a hundred others. Whatever thoughts buzzed beneath her tender scalp, they were a mystery to him. And his to her, presumably.

"It's a spiral," she said.

"What is?"

"The Pools. It's designed like a spiral. Look."

He stood up to get a bird's-eye view of the ground plan as she traced a route through the passageways with her index finger. She was right. Though the imperatives of the architects' brief had muddied the clarity of the image, there was indeed a rough spiral built into the maze of corridors and rooms. Her circling fingers drew tighter and yet tighter loops as it described the shape. At last it came to rest on the large pool, the locked pool. He stared at the plan in silence. Without her pointing it out he knew he could have looked at the design for a week and never seen the underlying structure.

Carole decided she would not stay the night. It was not, she tried to explain at the door, that things between them were over; only that she valued their intimacy too much to misuse it as bandaging. He half grasped the point; she too pictured them as wounded animals. At least they had some metaphorical life in common.

He was not unused to sleeping alone. In many ways he preferred to be solitary in his bed than to share it with someone, even Carole. But tonight he wanted her with him; not her, even, but *somebody*. He felt sourcelessly fretful, like a child. When sleep came it fled again, as if in fear of dreams.

Sometime toward dawn he got up, preferring wakefulness to that wretched sleep-hopping, wrapped his dressing gown around his shivering body, and went through to brew himself some tea. The ground plan was still spread on the coffee table where they had left it from the night before. Sipping the warm sweet Assam, he stood and pondered over it. Now that Carole had pointed it out, all he could concentrate upon—despite the clutter of marginalia that demanded his attention—was the spiral, that undisputable evidence of a hidden hand at work beneath the apparent chaos of the maze. It seized his eye and seduced it into following its unremitting route, round and round, tighter and tighter; and toward *what?* A locked swimming pool.

Tea drunk, he returned to bed; this time, fatigue got the better of his nerves and the sleep he'd been denied washed over him. He was wakened at seven-fifteen by Carole, who was phoning before she went to work to apologize for the previous night.

"I don't want everything to go wrong between us, Jerry. You do know that, don't you? You know you're precious to me."

He couldn't take love talk in the morning. What seemed

romantic at midnight struck him as ridiculous at dawn. He answered her declarations of commitment as best he could, and arranged to see her the following evening. Then he returned to his pillow.

•

Scarcely a quarter-hour had passed since he'd visited the Pools without Ezra Garvey thinking of the girl he'd glimpsed in the corridor. Her face had come back to him during dinner with his wife and sex with his mistress. So untrammeled, that face, so bright with possibilities.

Garvey thought of himself as a woman's man. Unlike most of his fellow potentates, whose consorts were a convenience best paid to be absent when not required for some specific function, Garvey enjoyed the company of the opposite sex. Their voices, their perfume, their laughter. His greed for their proximity knew few bounds; they were precious creatures whose company he was willing to spend small fortunes to secure. His jacket was therefore weighed down with money and expensive trinkets when he returned, that morning, to Leopold Road.

The pedestrians on the street were too concerned with keeping their head dry (a cold and steady drizzle had fallen since dawn) to notice the man on the step standing under a black umbrella while another bent to the business of undoing the padlock. Chandaman was an expert with locks. The shackle snapped open within seconds. Garvey lowered his umbrella and slipped into the vestibule.

"Wait here," he instructed Chandaman. "And close the door."

"Yes, sir."

"If I need you, I'll shout. You got the torch?"

Chandaman produced the flashlight from his jacket. Garvey took it, switched it on, and disappeared down the corridor. Either it was substantially colder outside than it had been the day before yesterday, or else the interior was hot. He unbuttoned his jacket, and loosened his tightly knotted tie. He welcomed the heat, reminding him as it did of the sheen on the dream girl's skin, of the heat-languored look in her dark eyes. He advanced down the corridor, splashing the flashlight's beam off the tiles. His sense of direction had always been good; it took him only a short time to find his way to the spot outside the large pool where he had encountered the girl. There he stood still and listened.

Garvey was a man used to looking over his shoulder. All his professional life, whether in or out of prison, he had needed to watch for the assassin at his back. Such ceaseless vigilance had made him sensitive to the least sign of human presence. Sounds another man might have ignored played a warning tattoo upon his eardrum. But here? Nothing. Silence in the corridors; silence in the sweating anterooms and the Turkish baths; silence in every tiled enclave from one end of the building to the other. And yet he knew he was not alone. When five senses failed him a sixth—belonging, perhaps, more to the beast in him than the sophisticate his expensive suit spoke of—sensed presences. This faculty had saved his hide more than once. Now, he hoped, it would guide him into the arms of beauty.

Trusting to instinct, he extinguished the light and headed off down the corridor from which the girl had first emerged, feeling his way along the walls. His quarry's presence tantalized him. He suspected she was a mere wall away, keeping pace with him along some secret passage he had no access to. The thought of this stalking pleased him. She and he, alone in this sweating maze, playing a game that both knew must end in capture. He moved stealthily, his pulse ticking off the seconds of the chase at neck and wrist and groin. His crucifix was glued to his breast bone with perspiration.

At last, the corridor divided. He halted. There was precious little light: what there was etched the tunnels deceptively. Impossible to judge distance. But trusting to his instinct, he turned left and followed his nose. Almost immediately, a door. It was open, and he walked through into a larger space; or so he guessed from the muted sound of his footsteps. Again, he stood still. This time, his straining ears were rewarded with a sound. Across the room from him, the soft pad of naked feet on the tiles. Was it his imagination, or did he even glimpse the girl, her body carved from the gloom, paler than the surrounding darkness, and smoother? Yes; it was she. He almost called out after her, and then thought better of it. Instead he went in silent pursuit, content to play her game for as long as it pleased her. Crossing the room, he stepped through another door which let on to a further tunnel. The air here was much warmer than anywhere else in the building, clammy and ingratiating as it pressed itself upon him. A moment's anxiety caught his throat: that he was neglecting every article of an autocrat's faith, putting his head so willingly into this warm noose. It could so easily be a setup: the girl, the chase. Around the next corner the breasts and the beauty might be gone, and there would be a knife at his heart. And yet he *knew* this wasn't so; *knew* that the footfall ahead was a woman's, light and lithe; that the swelter that brought new tides of sweat from him could nurture only softness and passivity here. No knife could prosper in such heat: its edge would soften, its ambition go neglected. He was safe.

Ahead, the footsteps had halted. He halted too. There was light from somewhere, though its source was not apparent. He licked his lips, tasting salt, then advanced. Beneath his fingers the tiles were glossed with water; under his heels, they were slick. Anticipation mounted in him with every step.

Now the light was brightening. It was not day. Sunlight had no route into this sanctum; this was more like moonlight— soft-edged, evasive—though that too must be exiled here, he thought. Whatever its origins, by it he finally set eyes on the girl; or rather, on *a* girl, for it was not the same he had seen two days before. Naked she was, young she was; but in all other respects different. He caught a glance from her before she fled from him down the corridor and turned a corner. Puzzlement now lent piquancy to the chase: not one but two girls, occupying this secret place. *Why?*

He looked behind him, to be certain his escape route lay open should he wish to retreat, but his memory, befuddled by the scented air, refused a clear picture of the way he'd come. A twinge of concern checked his exhilaration, but he refused to succumb to it, and pressed on, following the girl to the end of the corridor and turning left after her. The passageway ran for a short way before making another left; the girl even now was disappearing around that corner. Dimly aware that these gyrations were becoming tighter as he turned upon himself and upon himself again, he went where she led, panting now with the breath-quenching air and the insistence of the chase.

Suddenly, as he turned one final corner, the heat became smotheringly close, and the passageway delivered him out into a small, dimly lit chamber. He unbuttoned the top of his shirt; the veins on the back of his hands stood out like cord; he was aware of how his heart and lungs were laboring. But, he was relieved to see, the chase finished here. The object of his pursuit was standing with her back to him across the chamber, and at the sight of her smooth back and exquisite buttocks his claustrophobia evaporated.

"Girl . . . ," he panted. "You led me quite a chase."

She seemed not to hear him, or, more likely, was extending the game to its limits out of waywardness.

He started across the slippery tiles toward her.

"I'm talking to you."

As he came within half a dozen feet of her, she turned. It was not the girl he had just pursued through the corridor, not indeed the one he had seen two days before. This creature was another altogether. His gaze rested on her unfamiliar face a few seconds only, however, before sliding giddily down to meet the child she held in her arms. It was suckling like any newborn babe, pulling at her young breast with no little hunger. But in his four and a half decades of life Garvey's eyes had never seen a creature its like. Nausea rose in him. To see the girl giving suck was surprise enough, but to such a *thing*, such an outcast of any tribe, human or animal, was almost more than his stomach could stand. Hell itself had offspring more embraceable.

"What in Christ's name—?"

The girl stared at Garvey's alarm, and a wave of laughter broke over her face. He shook his head. The child in her arms uncurled a puckered limb and clamped it to its comforter's bosom so as to get better purchase. The gesture lashed Garvey's disgust into rage. Ignoring the girl's protests he snatched the abomination from her arms, holding it long enough to feel the glistening sac of its body squirm in his grasp, then flung it as hard as he could against the far wall of the chamber. As it struck the tiles it cried out, its complaint ending almost as soon as it began, only to be taken up instantly by the mother. She ran across the room to where the child lay, its apparently boneless body split open by the impact. One of its limbs, of which it possessed at least half a dozen, attempted to reach up to touch her sobbing face. She gathered the thing up into her arms; threads of shiny fluid ran across her belly and into her groin.

Out beyond the chamber something gave voice. Garvey had no doubt of its cue; it was answering the death-cry of the child, and the rising wail of its mother—but this sound was more distressing than either. Garvey's imagination was an impoverished faculty. Beyond his dreams of wealth and women lay a wasteland. Yet now, at the sound of that voice, the wasteland bloomed, and gave forth horrors he'd believed himself incapable of conceiving. Not portraits of monsters, which, at the best, could be no more than assemblies of experienced phenomena. What his mind created was more *feeling* than sight; belonged to his marrow, not to his mind. All certainty trembled—masculinity, power; the twin imperatives of dread and reason—all turned their collars up and denied knowledge of him. He shook, afraid as only dreams made him afraid, while the cry went on and on. Then he turned his back on the chamber, and ran, the light throwing his shadow in front of him down the dim corridor.

His sense of direction had deserted him. At the first intersection, and then at the second, he made an error. A few yards on he realized his mistake and tried to double back, but merely exacerbated the confusion. The corridors all looked alike: the same tiles, the same half-light, each fresh corner he turned either led him into a chamber he had not passed through or complete cul-de-sacs. His panic spiraled. The wailing had now ceased; he was alone with his rasping breath and half-spoken curses. Coloqhoun was responsible for this torment, and Garvey swore he would have its purpose beaten out of the man even if he had to break every bone in Coloqhoun's body personally. He clung to thoughts of that beating as he ran on; it was his only comfort. Indeed so preoccupied did he become with thought of the agonies he'd make Coloqhoun suffer he failed to realize that he had traced his way round in a circle and was running back *toward* the light until his sliding heels delivered him into a familiar chamber. The child lay on the floor, dead and discarded. Its mother was nowhere to be seen.

Garvey halted, and took stock of his situation. If he went back the way he'd come the route would only confound him again; if he went ahead, through the chamber and toward the light, he might cut the Gordian knot and be delivered back to his starting point. The swift wit of the solution pleased him. Cautiously, he crossed the chamber to the door on the other side and peered through. Another short corridor presented itself, and beyond that a door that let on to an open space. The pool! Surely the pool!

He threw caution to the wind and moved out of the chamber and along the passage.

With every step he took, the heat intensified. His head

thumped with it. He pressed on to the end of the passageway, and out into the arena beyond.

The large pool had not been drained, unlike the smaller. Rather, it was full almost to brimming—not with clear water, but with a scummy broth that steamed even in the heat of the interior. *This* was the source of the light. The water in the pool gave off a phosphorescence that tinged everything—the tiles, the diving board, the changing rooms (himself, no doubt)—with the same fulvous wash.

He scanned the scene in front of him. There was no sign of the women. His route to the exit lay unchallenged; nor could he see sign of padlock or chains on the double doors. He began toward them. His heel slid on the tiles, and he glanced down briefly to see that he had crossed a trail of fluid—difficult, in the bewitched light, to make out its color—that either ended at the water's edge, or began there.

He looked back toward the water, curiosity getting the better of him. The steam swirled; an eddy toyed with the scum. And there! His eye caught sight of a dark, anonymous shape sliding beneath the skin of the water. He thought of the creature he'd killed; of its formless body and the dangling loops of its limbs. Was this another of that species? The liquid brightness lapped against the poolside at his feet; continents of scum broke into archipelagoes. Of the swimmer, there was no sign.

Irritated, he looked away from the water. He was no longer alone. Three girls appeared from somewhere and were moving down the edge of the pool toward him. One he recognized as the girl he had first seen here. She was wearing a dress, unlike her sisters. One of her breasts was bared. She looked at him gravely as she approached; by her side she trailed a rope, decorated along its length with stained ribbons tied in limp but extravagant bows.

At the arrival of these three graces the fermenting waters of the pool were stirred into a frenzy as its occupants rose to meet the women. Garvey could see three or four restless forms teasing—but not breaking—the surface. He was caught between his instinct to take flight (the rope, though prettified, was still a rope) and the desire to linger and see what the pool contained. He glanced toward the door. He was within ten yards of it. A quick dash and he'd be out into the cool air of the corridor. From there, Chandaman was within calling distance.

The girls stood a few feet from him and watched him. He returned their looks. All the desires that had brought him here had taken heel. He no longer wanted to cup the breasts of these creatures, or dabble at the intersection of their gleaming thighs. These women were not what they seemed. Their quietness wasn't docility but a drug-trance; their nakedness wasn't sensuality but a horrid indifference that offended him. Even their youth, and all it brought—the softness of their skins, the gloss of their hair—even that was somehow corrupt. When the girl in the dress reached out and touched his sweating face, Garvey made a small cry of disgust, as if he'd been licked by a snake. She was not fazed by his response but stepped closer to him still, her eyes fixed on his, smelling not of perfume like his mistress but of fleshliness. Affronted as he was, he could not turn away. He stood, meeting the slut's eyes, as she kissed his cheek, and the beribboned rope was wrapped around his neck.

•

Jerry called Garvey's office at half-hour intervals through the day. At first he was told that he was out of the office and would be available later that afternoon. As the day wore on, however, the message changed. Garvey was not going to be in the office at all that day, Jerry was informed. Mr. Garvey is feeling unwell, the secretary told him; he has gone home to rest. Please call again tomorrow. Jerry left with her the message that he had secured the ground plan to the Pools and would be delighted to meet and discuss their plans at Mr. Garvey's convenience.

Carole called in the late afternoon.

"Shall we go out tonight?" she said. "Maybe a film?"

"What do you want to see?" he said.

"Oh, I hadn't really thought that far. We'll talk about it this evening, shall we?"

They ended up going to a French movie, which seemed, as far as Jerry could grasp, completely lacking in plot; it was simply a series of dialogues between characters discussing their traumas and their aspirations, the former being in direct proportion to the failure of the latter. It left him feeling torpid.

"You didn't like it . . ."

"Not much. All that browbeating."

"And no shoot-out."

She smiled to herself.

"What's so funny?"

"Nothing."

"Don't say nothing."

She shrugged. "I was just smiling, that's all. Can't I smile?"

"Jesus. All this conversation needs is subtitles."

They walked along Oxford Street a little way.

"Do you want to eat?" he said as they came to the head of Poland Street. "We could go to the Red Fort."

"No thanks. I hate eating late."

"For Christ's sake, let's not argue about a bloody film."

"Who's arguing?"

"You're so infuriating—"

"That's something we've got in common, anyhow," she returned. Her neck was flushed.

"You said this morning—"

"What?"

"About us not losing each other—"

"That was this morning," she said, eyes steely. And then, suddenly: "You don't give a *fuck*, Jerry. Not about me, not about anybody."

She stared at him, almost defying him to respond. When he failed to, she seemed curiously satisfied.

"Goodnight," she said, and began to walk away from him. He watched her take five, six, seven steps from him, the deepest part of him wanting to call after her, but a dozen irrelevancies—pride, fatigue, inconvenience—blocked his doing so. What eventually uprooted him, and put her name on his lips, was the thought of an empty bed tonight; of the sheets warm only where he lay, and chilly as hell to left and right of him.

"Carole."

She didn't turn; her step didn't even falter. He had to trot to catch up with her, conscious that this scene was probably entertaining the passersby.

"Carole." He caught hold of her arm. Now she stopped. When he moved round to face her he was shocked to see that she was crying. This discomfited him; he hated her tears only marginally less than his own.

"I surrender," he said, trying a smile. "The film was a masterpiece. How's that?"

She refused to be soothed by his antics; her face was swollen with unhappiness.

"Don't," he said. "Please don't. I'm not..." (Very good at apologies, he wanted to say, but he was so bad at them he couldn't even manage that much.)

"Never mind," she said softly. She wasn't angry, he saw; only miserable.

"Come back to the flat."

"I don't want to."

"*I* want you to," he replied. That at least was sincerely meant. "I don't like talking in the street."

He hailed a cab, and they made their way back to Kentish Town, keeping their silence. Halfway up the stairs to the door of the flat Carole said, "Foul perfume."

There was a strong, acidic smell lingering on the stairs.

"Somebody's been up here," he said, suddenly anxious, and

hurried on up the flight to the front door of his flat. It was open, the lock had been unceremoniously forced, the wood of the doorjamb splintered. He cursed.

"What's wrong?" Carole asked, following him up the stairs.

"Break-in."

He stepped into the flat and switched on the light. The interior was chaos. The whole flat had been comprehensively trashed. Everywhere, petty acts of vandalism—pictures smashed, pillows de-gutted, furniture reduced to timber. He stood in the middle of the turmoil and shook, while Carole went from room to room, finding the same thorough destruction in each.

"This is personal, Jerry."

He nodded.

"I'll call the police," she volunteered. "You find out what's missing."

He did as he was told, white-faced. The blow of this invasion numbed him. As he walked listlessly through the flat to survey the pandemonium—turning broken items over, pushing drawers back into place—he found himself imagining the intruders about their business, laughing as they worked through his clothes and keepsakes. In the corner of his bedroom he found a heap of his photographs. They had urinated on them.

"The police are on their way," Carole told him. "They said not to touch anything."

"Too late," he murmured.

"What's missing?"

"Nothing," he told her. All the valuables—the stereo and video equipment, his credit cards, his few items of jewelry— were there. Only then did he remember the ground plan. He returned to the living room and proceeded to root through the wreckage, but he knew damn well he wasn't going to find it.

"Garvey," he said.

"What about him?"

"He came for the ground plan of the Pools. Or sent someone."

"Why?" Carole replied, looking at the chaos. "You were going to give it to him anyway."

Jerry shook his head. "You were the one who warned me to stay clear—"

"I never expected anything like this."

"That makes two of us."

The police came and went, offering faint apologies for the fact that they thought an arrest unlikely. "There's a lot of vandalism around at the moment," the officer said. "There's nobody in downstairs..."

"No. They're away."

"Last hope, I'm afraid. We're getting calls like this all the time. You're insured?"

"Yes."

"Well, that's something."

Throughout the interview Jerry kept silent on his suspicions though he was repeatedly tempted to point the finger. There was little purpose in accusing Garvey at this juncture. For one, Garvey would have alibis prepared; for another, what would unsubstantiated accusations do but further inflame the man's unreason?

"What will you do?" Carole asked him when the police had picked up their shrugs and left.

"I don't know. I can't even be certain it *was* Garvey. One minute he's all sweetness and light; the next this. How do I deal with a mind like that?"

"You don't. You leave it alone," she replied. "Do you want to stay here, or go over to my place?"

"Stay," he said.

They made a perfunctory attempt to restore the former status quo—righting the furniture that was not too crippled to stand and clearing up the broken glass. Then they turned the slashed mattress over, located two unmutilated cushions, and went to bed.

She wanted to make love, but that reassurance, like so much of his life of late, was doomed to failure. There was no making good between the sheets what had been so badly soured out of them. His anger made him rough, and his roughness in turn angered her. She frowned beneath him, her kisses unwilling and tight. Her reluctance only spurned him on to fresh crassness.

"Stop," she said, as he was about to enter her. "I don't want this."

He did, and badly. He pushed before she could further her objections.

"I said *don't*, Jerry."

He shut out her voice. He was half as heavy again as she. "*Stop*."

He closed his eyes. She told him again to stop, this time with real fury, but he just thrust harder—the way she'd ask him to sometimes, when the heat was really on—beg him to, even. But now she only swore at him, and threatened, and every word she said made him more intent not to be cheated of this, though he felt nothing at his groin but fullness and discomfort, and the urge to be finished.

She began to fight, raking at his back with her nails, and pulling at his hair to unclamp his face from her neck. It passed through his head as he labored that she would hate him for this, and on that, at least, they would be of one accord, but the thought was soon lost to sensation.

The poison passed, he rolled off her.

"Bastard," she said.

His back stung. When he got up from the bed he left blood on the sheets. Digging through the chaos in the living room he located an unbroken bottle of whiskey. The glasses, however, were all smashed, and out of absurd fastidiousness he didn't want to drink from the bottle. He squatted against the wall, his back chilled, feeling neither wretched nor proud. The front door opened, and was slammed. He waited, listening to Carole's feet on the stairs. Then tears came, though these too he felt utterly detached from. Finally, the bout dispatched, he went through into the kitchen, found a cup, and drank himself senseless.

•

Garvey's study was an impressive room; he'd had it fashioned after that of a tax lawyer he'd known, the walls lined with books purchased by the yard, the color of carpet and paint work alike muted, as though by an accrual of cigar smoke and learning. When he found sleep difficult, as he did now, he would retire to the study, sit on his leather-backed chair behind a vast desk, and dream of legitimacy. Not tonight, however; tonight his thoughts were otherwise preoccupied. Always, however much he might try to turn to another route, they went back to Leopold Road.

He remembered little of what had happened at the Pools. That in itself was distressing; he had always prided himself upon the acuteness of his memory. Indeed his recall of faces seen and favors done had in no small measure helped him to his present power. Of the hundreds in his employ he boasted that there was not a doorkeeper or a cleaner he could not address by Christian name.

But of the events at Leopold Road, barely thirty-six hours old, he had only the vaguest recollection; of the women closing upon him, and the rope tightening around his neck; of their leading him along the lip of the pool to some chamber the vileness of which had practically snatched his senses away. What had followed his arrival there moved in his memory like those forms in the filth of the pool: obscure, but horribly distressing. There had been humiliation and horrors, hadn't there? Beyond that, he remembered nothing.

He was not a man to kowtow to such ambiguities without argument, however. If there were mysteries to be uncovered here, then he would do so, and take the consequence of revelation.

His first offensive had been sending Chandaman and Fryer to tear up Coloqhoun's place. If, as he suspected, this whole enterprise was some elaborate trap devised by his enemies, then Coloqhoun was involved in its setting. No more than a front man, no doubt; certainly not the mastermind. But Garvey was satisfied that the destruction of Coloqhoun's goods and chattels would warn his masters of his intent to fight. It had borne other fruit too. Chandaman had returned with the ground plan of the Pools; they were spread on Garvey's desk now. He had traced his route through the complex time and again, hoping that his memory might be jogged. He had been disappointed.

Weary, he got up and went to the study window. The garden behind the house was vast and painstakingly tended. He could see little of the immaculate borders at the moment, however; the starlight barely described the world outside. All he could see was his own reflection in the polished pane.

As he focused on it, his outline seemed to waver, and he felt a loosening in his lower belly, as if something had come unknotted there. He put his hand to his abdomen. It twitched, it trembled, and for an instant he was back in the Pools, and naked, and something lumpen moved in front of his eyes. He almost yelled, but stopped himself by turning away from the window and staring at the room; at the carpets and the books and the furniture; at sober, solid reality. Even then the images refused to leave his head entirely. The coils of his innards were still jittery.

It was several minutes before he could bring himself to look back at the reflection in the window. When at last he did all trace of the vacillation had disappeared. He would countenance no more nights like this, sleepless and haunted. With the first light of dawn came the conviction that today was the day to break Mr. Coloqhoun.

•

Jerry tried to call Carole at her office that morning. She was repeatedly unavailable. Eventually he simply gave up trying and turned his attentions to the Herculean task of restoring some order to the flat. He lacked the focus and the energy to do a good job, however. After a futile hour, in which he seemed not to have made more than a dent, he gave up. The chaos accurately reflected his opinion of himself. Best perhaps that it be left to lie.

Just before noon, he received a call.

"Mr. Coloqhoun? Mr. *Gerard* Coloqhoun?"

"That's right."

"My name's Fryer. I'm calling on behalf of Mr. Garvey."

"Oh?"

Was this to gloat, or threaten further mischief?

"Mr. Garvey was expecting some proposals from you," Fryer said.

"Proposals?"

"He's very enthusiastic about the Leopold Road project, Mr. Coloqhoun. He feels there's substantial monies to be made."

Jerry said nothing; this palaver confounded him.

"Mr. Garvey would like another meeting as soon as possible."

"Yes?"

"At the Pools. There's a few architectural details he'd like to show his colleagues."

"I see."

"Would you be available later on today?"

"Yes. Of course."

"Four-thirty?"

The conversation more or less ended there, leaving Jerry mystified. There had been no trace of enmity in Fryer's manner; no hint, however subtle, of bad blood between the two parties. Perhaps, as the police had suggested, the events of the previous night *had* been the work of anonymous vandals—the theft of the ground plan a whim of theirs. His depressed spirits rose. All was not lost.

He rang Carole again, buoyed up by this turn of events.

This time he did not take the repeated excuses of her colleagues but insisted on speaking to her. Finally, she picked up the phone.

"I don't want to talk to you, Jerry. Just go to hell."

"Just hear me out—"

She slammed the receiver down before he said another word. He rang back immediately. When she answered and heard his voice, she seemed baffled that he was so eager to make amends.

"Why are you even trying?" she said. "Jesus Christ, what's the use?" He could hear the tears in her throat.

"I want you to understand how sick I feel. Let me make it right. *Please* let me make it right."

She didn't reply to his appeal.

"Don't put the phone down. Please don't. I know it was unforgivable. Jesus, I know..."

Still she kept her silence.

"Just think about it, will you? Give me a chance to put things right. Will you do that?"

Very quietly, she said, "I don't see the use."

"May I call you tomorrow?"

He heard her sigh.

"May I?"

"Yes. Yes."

The line went dead.

•

He set out for his meeting at Leopold Road with a full three-quarters of an hour to spare, but halfway to his destination the rain came on, great spots of it which defied the best efforts of his windshield wipers. The traffic slowed; he crawled for half a mile, with only the rear lights of the vehicle ahead visible through the deluge. The minutes ticked by, and his anxiety mounted. By the time he edged his way out of the fouled-up traffic to find another route, he was already late. There was nobody waiting on the steps of the Pools, but Garvey's powder-blue Rover was parked a little way down the road. There was no sign of the chauffeur. Jerry found a place to park on the opposite side of the road and crossed through the rain. It was a matter of fifty yards from the door of the car to that of the Pools, but by the time he reached his destination he was drenched and breathless. The door was open. Garvey had clearly manipulated the lock and slipped out of the downpour. Jerry ducked inside.

Garvey was not in the vestibule, but somebody was. A man of Jerry's height but with half again the width. He was wearing leather gloves. His face, but for the absence of seams, might have been of the same material.

"Coloqhoun?"

"Yes."

"Mr. Garvey is waiting for you inside."

"Who are you?"

"Chandaman," the man replied. "Go right in."

There was a light at the far end of the corridor. Jerry pushed open the glass-paneled vestibule doors and walked down toward it. Behind him, he heard the front door snap closed, and then the echoing tread of Garvey's lieutenant.

Garvey was talking with another man, shorter than Chandaman, who was holding a sizable flashlight. When the pair heard Jerry approach they looked his way; their conversation abruptly ceased. Garvey offered no welcoming comment or hand but merely said, "About time."

"The rain . . . ," Jerry began, then thought better of offering a self-evident explanation.

"You'll catch your death," the man with the flashlight said. Jerry immediately recognized the dulcet tones of:

"Fryer."

"The same," the man returned.

"Pleased to meet you."

They shook hands, and as they did so Jerry caught sight of Garvey, who was staring at him as though in search of a second head. The man didn't say anything for what seemed like half a minute, but simply studied the growing discomfort on Jerry's face.

"I'm not a stupid man," Garvey said eventually.

The statement, coming out of nowhere, begged response.

"I don't even believe you're the main man in all of this," Garvey went on. "I'm prepared to be charitable."

"What's this about?"

"Charitable," Garvey repeated, "because I think you're out of your depth. Isn't that right?"

Jerry just frowned.

"I think that's right," Fryer replied.

"I don't think you understand how much trouble you're in even now, do you?" Garvey said.

Jerry was suddenly uncomfortably aware of Chandaman standing behind him, and of his own utter vulnerability.

"But I don't think ignorance should ever be bliss," Garvey was saying. "I mean, even if you don't *understand*, that doesn't make you exempt, does it?"

"I haven't a clue what you're talking about," Jerry protested mildly. Garvey's face, by the light of the flashlight, was drawn and pale; he looked in need of a holiday.

"This place," Garvey returned. "I'm talking about *this place*. The women you put in here . . . for my benefit. What's it all about, Coloqhoun? That's all I want to know. *What's it all about?*"

Jerry shrugged lightly. Each word Garvey uttered merely perplexed him more, but the man had already told him ignorance would not be considered a legitimate excuse. Perhaps a question was the wisest reply.

"You saw women here?" he said.

"Whores, more like," Garvey responded. His breath smelled of last week's cigar ash. "Who are you working for, Coloqhoun?"

"For myself. The deal I offered—"

THE MADONNA · 161

"Forget your fucking deal," Garvey said. "I'm not interested in deals."

"I see," Jerry replied. "Then I don't see any point in this conversation." He took a half-step away from Garvey, but the man's arm shot out and caught hold of his rain-sodden coat.

"I didn't tell you to go," Garvey said.

"I've got business—"

"Then it'll have to wait," the other replied, scarcely relaxing his grip. Jerry knew that if he tried to shrug off Garvey and make a dash for the front door he'd be stopped by Chandaman before he made three paces. If, on the other hand, he didn't try to escape—

"I don't much like your sort," Garvey said, removing his hand. "Smart brats with an eye to the main chance. Think you're so damn clever, just because you've got a fancy accent and a silk tie. Let me tell you something"—he jabbed his finger at Jerry's throat—"I don't give a shit about you. I just want to know who you work for. Understand?"

"I already told you—"

"*Who do you work for?*" Garvey insisted, punctuating each word with a fresh jab. "Or you're going to feel very sick."

"For Christ's sake—I'm not working for anybody. And I don't know anything about any women."

"Don't make it worse than it already is," Fryer advised him with feigned concern.

"I'm telling the truth."

"I think the man wants to be hurt," Fryer said. Chandaman gave a joyless laugh. "Is that what you want?"

"Just name some names," Garvey said. "Or we're going to break your legs." The threat, unequivocal as it was, did nothing for Jerry's clarity of mind. He could think of no way out of this but to continue to insist upon his innocence. If he named some fictitious employer the lie would be uncovered in moments, and the consequences could only be worse for the attempted deception.

"Check my credentials," he pleaded. "You've got the resources. Dig around. I'm not a company man, Garvey; I never have been."

Garvey's eye left Jerry's face for a moment and moved to his shoulder. Jerry grasped the significance of the sign a heartbeat too late to prepare himself for the blow to his kidneys from the man at his back. He pitched forward, but before he could collide with Garvey, Chandaman had snatched at his collar and was throwing him against the wall. He doubled up, the pain blinding him to all other thoughts. Vaguely, he heard Garvey asking him again who his boss was. He shook his head. His skull was full of ball bearings; they rattled between his ears.

"Jesus . . . Jesus . . . ," he said, groping for some word of defense to keep another beating at bay, but he was hauled upright before any presented itself. The flashlight was turned on him. He was ashamed of the tears that were rolling down his cheeks.

"*Names,*" said Garvey.

The ball bearings rattled on.

"Again," said Garvey, and Chandaman was moving in to give his fists further exercise. Garvey called him off as Jerry came close to passing out. The leather face withdrew.

"Stand up when I'm talking to you," Garvey said.

Jerry attempted to oblige, but his body was less than willing to comply. It trembled, it felt fit to die.

"Stand up," Fryer reiterated, moving between Jerry and his tormentor to prod the point home. Now, in close proximity, Jerry smelled that acidic scent Carole had caught on the stairs: it was Fryer's cologne.

"Stand up!" the man insisted.

Jerry raised a feeble hand to shield his face from the blinding beam. He could not see any of the trio's faces, but he was dimly aware that Fryer was blocking Chandaman's access to him. To Jerry's right, Garvey struck a match, and applied the flame to a cigar. A moment presented itself: Garvey was occupied, the thug stymied. Jerry took it.

Ducking down beneath the beam he broke from his place against the wall, contriving to knock the flashlight from Fryer's hand as he did so. The light-source clattered across the tiles and went out.

In the sudden darkness, Jerry made a stumbling bid for freedom. Behind him, he heard Garvey curse; heard Chandaman and Fryer collide as they scrabbled for the fallen flashlight. He began to edge his way along the wall to the end of the corridor. There was evidently no safe route past his tormentors to the front door; his only hope lay in losing himself in the networks of corridors that lay ahead.

He reached a corner, and made a right, vaguely remembering that this led him off the main hallways and into the service corridors. The beating that he'd taken, though interrupted before it could incapacitate, had rendered him breathless and bruised. He felt every step he took as a sharp pain in his lower abdomen and back. When he slipped on the slimy tiles, the impact almost made him cry out.

At his back, Garvey was shouting again. The flashlight had been located. Its light bounced down the labyrinth to find him. Jerry hurried on, glad of the murky illumination, but not of its source. They would follow, and quickly. If, as Carole had said, the place was a simple spiral, the corridors describing a relentless loop with no way out of the configuration, he was lost. But he was committed. Head giddied by the mounting heat, he moved on, praying to find a fire exit that would give him passage out of this trap.

"He went this way," Fryer said. "He must have done."

Garvey nodded; it was indeed the likeliest route for Coloqhoun to have taken. Away from the light and into the labyrinth.

"Shall we go after him?" Chandaman said. The man was fairly salivating to finish the beating he'd started. "He can't have got far."

"No," said Garvey. Nothing, not even the promise of knighthood, would have induced him to follow.

Fryer had already advanced down the passageway a few yards, shining the beam on the glistening walls.

"It's warm," he said.

Garvey knew all to well how warm it was. Such heat wasn't natural, not for England. This was a temperate isle; that was why he had never set foot off it. The sweltering heat of other continents bred grotesqueries he wanted no sight of.

"What do we do?" Chandaman demanded. "Wait for him to come out?"

Garvey pondered this. The smell from the corridor was beginning to distress him. His innards were churning, his skin was crawling. Instinctively, he put his hand to his groin. His manhood had shrunk in trepidation.

"No," he said suddenly.

"No?"

"We're not waiting."

"He can't stay in there forever."

"I said *no!*" He hadn't anticipated how profoundly the sweat of the place would upset him. Irritating as it was to let Coloqhoun slip away like this, he knew that if he stayed here much longer he risked losing his self-control.

"You two can wait for him at his flat," he told Chandaman. "He'll have to come home sooner or later."

"Damn shame," Fryer muttered as he emerged from the passageway. "I like a chase."

•

Perhaps they weren't following. It was several minutes now since Jerry had heard the voices behind him. His heart had stopped its furious pumping. Now, with the adrenaline no longer giving speed to his heels and distracting his muscles from their bruising, his pace slowed to a crawl. His body protested at even that.

When the agonies of taking another step became too much

he slid down the wall and sat slumped across the passageway. His rain-drenched clothes clung to his body and about his throat; he felt both chilled and suffocated by them. He pulled at the knot of his tie, and then unbuttoned his jacket and his shirt. The air in the labyrinth was warm on his skin. Its touch was welcome.

He closed his eyes and made a studied attempt to mesmerize himself out of this pain. What was feeling but a trick of the nerve-endings? There were techniques for dislocating the mind from the body and leaving agonies behind. But no sooner had his lids closed than he heard muted sounds somewhere nearby. Footsteps; the lull of voices. It wasn't Garvey and his associates: the voices were female. Jerry raised his leaden head and opened his eyes. Either he had become used to the darkness in his few moments of meditation or else a light had crept into the passageway; it was surely the latter.

He got to his feet. His jacket was dead weight, and he sloughed it off, leaving it to lie where he'd been squatting. Then he started in the direction of the light. The heat seemed to have risen considerably in the last few minutes: it gave him mild hallucinations. The walls seemed to have forsaken verticality, the air to have traded transparency for a shimmering aurora.

He turned a corner. The light brightened. Another corner, and he was delivered into a small tiled chamber, the heat of which took his breath away. He gasped like a stranded fish and peered across the chamber—the air thickening with every pulse-beat—at the door on the far side. The yellowish light through it was brighter still, but he could not summon the will to follow it a yard farther; the heat here had defeated him. Sensing that he was within an ace of unconsciousness, he put his hand out to support himself, but his palm slid on the slick tiles, and he fell, landing on his side. He could not prevent a shout spilling from him.

Groaning his misery, he tucked his legs up close to his body, and lay where he'd fallen. If Garvey had heard his yell, and sent his lieutenants in pursuit, then so be it. He was past caring.

The sound of movement reached him from across the chamber. Raising his head an inch from the floor he opened his eyes to a slit. A naked girl had appeared in the doorway opposite, or so his reeling senses informed him. Her skin shone as if oiled; here and there, on her breasts and thighs, were smudges of what might have been old blood. Not her blood, however. There was no wound to spoil her gleaming body.

The girl had begun to laugh at him, a light, easy laugh that made him feel foolish. Its musicality entranced him however, and he made an effort to get a better look at her. She had started to move across the chamber toward him, still laughing; and now he saw that there were others behind her. These were the women Garvey had babbled about; this the trap he had accused Jerry of setting.

"Who are you?" he murmured as the girl approached him. Her laughter faltered when she looked down at his pain-contorted features.

He attempted to sit upright, but his arms were numb, and he slid back to the tiles again. The woman had not answered his inquiry, nor did she make any attempt to help him. She simply stared down at him as a pedestrian might at a drunk in the gutter, her face unreadable. Looking up at her, Jerry felt his tenuous grip on consciousness slipping. The heat, his pain, and now this sudden eruption of beauty was too much for him. The distant women were dispersing into darkness, the entire chamber folding up like a magician's box until the sublime creature in front of him claimed his attention utterly. And now, at her silent insistence, his mind's eye seemed to be plucked from his head, and suddenly he was speeding over her skin, her flesh a landscape, each pore a pit, each hair a pylon. He was hers, utterly. She drowned him in her eyes, and flayed him with her lashes; she rolled him across her abdomen, and down the soft channel of her spine. She took him between her buttocks, and then up into her heat, and out again just as he thought he must burn alive. The velocity exhilarated him. He was aware that his body, somewhere below, was hyperventilating in its terror; but his imagination—careless of breath—went willingly where she sent him, looping like a bird, until he was thrown, ragged and dizzy, back into the cup of his skull. Before he could apply the fragile tool of reason to the phenomena he had just experienced, his eyes fluttered closed and he passed out.

•

The body does not need the mind. It has procedures aplenty—lungs to be filled and emptied, blood to be pumped and food profited from—none of which require the authority of thought. Only when one or more of these procedures falters does the mind become aware of the intricacy of the mechanism it inhabits. Coloqhoun's faint lasted only a few minutes, but when he came to he was aware of his body as he had seldom been before: as a trap. Its fragility was a trap; its shape, its size, its very gender was a trap. And there was no flying out of it; he was shackled to, or *in*, this wretchedness.

These thoughts came and went. In between them there were brief sights through which he fell giddily, and still briefer moments in which he glimpsed the world outside himself.

The women had picked him up. His head lolled; his hair dragged on the floor. I am a trophy, he thought in a more coherent instant. Then the darkness came again. And again he struggled to the surface, and now they were carrying him along the edge of the large pool. His nostrils were filled with contradictory scents, both delectable and fetid. From the corner of his lazy eye he could see water so bright it seemed to burn as it lapped the shores of the pool: and something else too—shadows moving in the brightness.

They mean to drown me, he thought. And then: I'm already drowning. He imagined water filling his mouth: imagined the forms he had glimpsed in the pool invading his throat and slipping into his belly. He struggled to vomit them back up, his body convulsing.

A hand was laid on his face. The palm was blissfully cool. "*Hush*," somebody murmured to him, and at the words his delusions melted away. He felt himself coaxed out of his terrors and into consciousness.

The hand had evaporated from his brow. He looked around the gloomy room for his savior, but his eyes didn't travel far. On the other side of this chamber—which looked to have been a communal shower-room—several pipes, set high in the wall, delivered solid arcs of water onto the tiles, where gutters channeled it away. A fine spray and the gushing of the fountains filled the air. Jerry sat up. There was movement behind the cascading veil of water: a shape too vast by far to be human. He peered through the drizzle to try to make sense of the folds of flesh. Was it an animal? There was a pungent smell in here that had something of the menagerie about it.

Moving with considerable caution so as not to arouse the beast's attention, Jerry attempted to stand up. His legs, however, were not the equal of his intention. All he could do was crawl a little way across the room on his hands and knees, and peer—one beast at another—through the veil.

He sensed that he was sensed; that the dark, recumbent creature had turned its eyes in his direction. Beneath its gaze, he felt his skin creep with gooseflesh, but he couldn't take his eyes off it. And then, as he squinted to scrutinize it better, a spark of phosphorescence began in its substance, and spread—fluttering waves of jaundiced light—up and across its tremendous form, revealing itself to Coloqhoun.

Not it; *she*. He knew indisputably that this creature was female, though it resembled no species or genus he knew of. As the ripples of luminescence moved through the creature's physique, it revealed with every fresh pulsation some new and phenomenal configuration. Watching her, Jerry thought of something slow and molten—glass, perhaps; or stone—its flesh extruded into elaborate forms and recalled again into the furnace to be remade. She had neither head nor limbs recognizable as such, but her contours were ripe with clusters of bright bubbles that might have been eyes, and she threw out here and there iridescent ribbons—slow, pastel flames—that seemed momentarily to ignite the very air.

Now the body issued a series of soft noises: scuttlings and sighs. He wondered if he was being addressed, and if so, how he was expected to respond. Hearing footfalls behind him, he glanced around at one of the women for guidance.

"Don't be afraid," she said.

"I'm not," he replied. It was the truth. The prodigy in front of him was electrifying but woke no fear in him.

"What is she?" he asked.

The woman stood close to him. Her skin, bathed by the shimmering light off the creature, was golden. Despite the circumstances—or perhaps because of them—he felt a tremor of desire.

"She is the Madonna. The Virgin Mother."

Mother? Jerry mouthed, swiveling his head back to look at the creature again. The waves of phosphorescence had ceased to break across her body. Now the light pulsed in one part of her anatomy only, and at this region, in rhythm with the pulse, the Madonna's substance was swelling and splitting. Behind him he heard further footsteps; and now whispers echoed about the chamber, and chiming laughter, and applause.

The Madonna was giving birth. The swollen flesh was opening; liquid light gushing; the smell of smoke and blood filled the shower room. A girl gave a cry, as if in sympathy with the Madonna. The applause mounted, and suddenly the slit spasmed and delivered the child—something between a squid and a shorn lamb—onto the tiles. The water from the pipes slapped it into consciousness immediately, and it threw back its head to look about it; its single eye vast and perfectly lucid.

It squirmed on the tiles for a few moments before the girl at Jerry's side stepped forward into the veil of water and picked it up. Its toothless mouth sought out her breast immediately. The girl delivered it to her tit.

"Not human . . . ," Jerry murmured. He had not prepared himself for a child so strange, and yet so unequivocally intelligent. "Are all . . . all the children like that?"

The surrogate mother gazed down at the sac of life in her arms. "No one is like another," she replied. "We feed them. Some die. Others live, and go their ways."

"Where, for God's sake?"

"To the water. To the sea. Into dreams."

She cooed to it. A fluted limb, in which light ran as it had in its parent, paddled the air with pleasure.

"And the father?"

"She needs no husband," the reply came. "She could make children from a shower of rain if she so desired."

Jerry looked back at the Madonna. All but the last vestige of light had been extinguished in her. The vast body threw out a tendril of saffron flame, which caught the cascade of water, and threw dancing patterns on the wall. Then it was still. When Jerry looked back for the mother and child, they had gone. Indeed all the women had gone but one. It was the girl who had first appeared to him. The smile she'd worn was on her face again as she sat across the room from him, her legs splayed. He gazed at the place between them, and then back at her face.

"What are you afraid of?" she asked.

"I'm not afraid."

"Then why don't you come to me?"

He stood up, and crossed the chamber to where she sat. Behind him, the water still slapped and ran on the tiles, and behind the fountains the Madonna murmured in her flesh. He was not intimidated by her presence. The likes of him was surely beneath the notice of such a creature. If she saw him

THE MADONNA · 171

at all she doubtless thought him ridiculous. Jesus! he was ridiculous even to himself. He had neither hope nor dignity to lose.

Tomorrow, all this would be a dream: the water, the children, the beauty who even now stood up to embrace him. Tomorrow he would think he had died for a day and visited a shower room for angels. For now, he would make what he could of the opportunity.

After they had made love, he and the smiling girl, when he tried to recall the specifics of the act, he could not be certain that he had performed at all. Only the vaguest memories remained to him, and they were not of her kisses, or of how they coupled, but of a dribble of milk from her breast and the way she murmured, "Never...never..." as they had entwined. When they were done, she was indifferent. There were no more words, no more smiles. She just left him alone in the drizzle of the chamber. He buttoned up his soiled trousers, and left the Madonna to her fecundity.

A short corridor led out of the shower room and into the large pool. It was, as he had vaguely registered when they had brought him into the presence of the Madonna, brimming. Her children played in the radiant water, their forms multitudinous. The women were nowhere to be seen, but the door to the outer corridor stood open. He walked through it, and had taken no more than half a dozen steps before it slid closed behind him.

•

Now, all too late, Ezra Garvey knew that returning to the Pools (even for an act of intimidation, which he had traditionally enjoyed) had been an error. It had re-opened a wound in him that he had hoped was near to healing; and it had brought memories of his second visit there, of the women and what they had displayed to him closer to the surface (memories which he had sought to clarify until he began to grasp their true nature). They had drugged him somehow, hadn't they?; and then, when he was weak and had lost all sense of propriety, they had exploited him for their entertainment. They had suckled him like a child, and made him their plaything. The memories of that merely perplexed him; but there were others, too deep to be distinguished quite, that *appalled*. Of some inner chamber, and of water falling in a curtain; of a darkness that was terrible, and a luminescence that was more terrible still.

The time had come, he knew, to trample these dreams underfoot and be done with such bafflement. He was a man who forgot neither favors done nor favors owed. A little before eleven he had two telephone conversations, to call some of those favors in. Whatever lived at Leopold Road Pools would prosper there no longer. Satisfied with his night's maneuvers, he went upstairs to bed.

He had drunk the best part of a bottle of schnapps since returning from the incident with Coloqhoun, chilled and uneasy. Now the spirit in his system caught up with him. His limbs felt heavy, his head heavier still. He did not even concern himself to undress, but lay down on his double bed for a few minutes to allow his senses to clear. When he next woke, it was 1:30 A.M.

He sat up. His belly was cavorting again; indeed his whole body seemed to be traumatized. He had seldom been ill in his forty-odd years: success had kept ailments at bay. But now he felt terrible. He had a headache which was near to blinding— he stumbled from his bedroom down to the kitchen more by aid of touch than sight. There he poured himself a glass of milk, sat down at the table, and put it to his lips. He did not drink however. His gaze had alighted on the hand that held his glass. He stared at it through a fog of pain. It didn't seem to be *his* hand: it was too fine, too smooth. He put the glass down, trembling, but it tipped over, the milk pooling on the teak tabletop and running off onto the floor.

He got to his feet, the sound of the milk dribbling onto the kitchen tiles awaking curious thoughts, and moved unsteadily through to his study. He needed to be with somebody: *anybody* would do. He picked up his telephone book and tried to make sense of the scrawlings on each page, but the numbers would not come clear. His panic was growing. Was this insanity? The delusion of his transformed hand, the unnatural sensations that were running through his body. He reached to unbutton his shirt, and in doing so his hand brushed another delusion, more absurd than the first. Fingers unwilling, he tore at the shirt, telling himself over and over that none of this was possible.

But the evidence was plain. He touched a body which was no longer his. There were still signs that the flesh and bone belonged to him—an appendix scar on his lower abdomen, a birthmark beneath his arm—but the substance of his body had been teased (was *being* teased still, even as he watched) into shapes that shamed him. He clawed at the forms that disfigured his torso, as if they might dissolve beneath his assault, but they merely bled.

In his time, Ezra Garvey had suffered much, almost all his sufferings self-inflicted. He had undergone periods of imprisonment; come close to serious physical wounding; had endured the deceptions of beautiful women. But those torments were nothing beside the anguish he felt now. He was not himself! His body had been taken from him while he slept and this changeling left in its place. The horror of it shattered his self-esteem, and left his sanity teetering.

Unable to hold back the tears, he began to pull at the belt of his trousers. Please God, he babbled, please God let me be whole still. He could barely see for the tears. He wiped them away, and peered at his groin. Seeing what deformities were in progress there, he roared until the windows rattled.

Garvey was not a man for prevarication. Deeds, he knew, were not best served by debate. He wasn't sure how this treatise on transformation had been written into his system, and he didn't much care. All he could think of was how many deaths of shame he would die if this vile condition ever saw the light of day. He returned to the kitchen, selected a large meat-knife from the drawer, then adjusted his clothing and left the house.

His tears had dried. They were wasted now, and he was not a wasteful man. He drove through the empty city down to the river and across Blackfriars Bridge. There he parked and walked down to the water's edge. The Thames was high and fast tonight, the tops of the waters were whipped white.

Only now, having come so far without examining his intentions too closely, did fear of extinction give him pause. He was a wealthy and influential man; were there not other routes out of this ordeal other than the one he had come headlong to? Pill peddlars who could reverse the lunacy that had seized his cells; surgeons who might slice off the offending parts and knit his lost self back together again? But how long would such solutions last? Sooner or later, the process would begin again: he knew it. He was beyond help.

A gust of wind blew spume up off the water. It rained against his face, and the sensation finally broke the seal on his forgetfulness. At last he remembered it all: the shower room, the spouts from the severed pipes beating on the floor, the heat, the women laughing and applauding. And finally, the thing that lived behind the water wall, a creature that was worse than any nightmare of womanhood his grieving mind had dredged up. He had fucked there, in the presence of that behemoth, and in the fury of the act—when he had momentarily forgotten himself—the bitches had worked this rapture upon him. No use for regrets. What was done, was done. At least he had made provision for the destruction of their lair. Now he would undo by self-surgery what they had contrived by magic, and so at last deny them sight of their handiwork.

The wind was cold, but his blood was hot. It came gushingly as he slashed at his body. The Thames received the libation with enthusiasm. It lapped at his feet; it whipped itself into eddies. He had not finished the job, however, when the loss of blood overcame him. No matter, he thought, as his knees buckled and he toppled into the water, no one will know me now but fishes. The prayer he offered up as the river closed over him was that death not be a woman.

•

Long before Garvey had awakened in the night, and discovered his body in rebellion, Jerry had left the Pools, got into his car, and attempted to drive home. He had not been the equal of that simple task, however. His eyes were bleary, his sense of direction confused. After a near accident at an intersection he parked the car and began to walk back to the flat. His memories of what had just happened to him were by no means clear, though the events were mere hours old. His head was full of strange associations. He walked in the solid world, but half dreaming. It was the sight of Chandaman and Fryer, waiting for him in the bedroom of his flat, that slapped him back into reality. He did not wait for them to greet him, but turned and ran. They had emptied his stock of spirits as they lay in ambush, and were slow to respond. He was down the stairs and gone from the house before they could give chase.

He walked to Carole's; she was not in. He didn't mind waiting. He sat on the front steps of her home for half an hour, and when the tenant of the top floor flat arrived talked his way into the comparative warmth of the house itself and kept vigil on the stairs. There he fell to dozing, and retraced his steps over the route he'd come, back to the intersection where he'd abandoned the car. A crowd of people were passing the place. "*Where are you going?*" he asked them. "*To see the yatches,*" they replied. "*What yatches are those?*" he wanted to know, but they were already drifting away, chattering. He walked on a while. The sky was dark, but the streets were illuminated nevertheless by a wash of blue and shadowless light. Just as he was about to come within sight of the Pools, he heard a splashing sound, and, turning a corner, discovered that the tide was coming in up Leopold Street. What sea was this? he inquired of the gulls overhead, for the salt tang in the air declared these waters as ocean, not river. Did it matter what sea it was, they returned? Weren't all seas *one* sea, finally? He stood and watched the wavelets creeping across the tarmac. Their advance, though gentle, overturned lamp posts, and so swiftly eroded the foundations of the buildings that they fell, silently, beneath the glacial tide. Soon the waves were around his feet. Fishes, tiny darts of silver, moved in the water.

"Jerry?"

Carole was on the stairs, staring at him.

"What the hell's happened to you?"

"I could have drowned," he said.

•

He told her about the trap Garvey had set at Leopold Road, and how he'd been beaten up; then of the thugs' presence at his own house. She offered cool sympathy. He said nothing about the chase through the spiral, or the women, or the something that he'd seen in the shower room. He couldn't have articulated it even if he'd wanted to: every hour that passed since he'd left the Pools he was less certain of having seen anything at all.

"Do you want to stay here?" she asked him when he'd finished his account.

"I thought you'd never ask."

"You'd better have a bath. Are you sure they didn't break any bones?"

"I think I'd feel it by now if they had."

No broken bones, perhaps; but he had not escaped unmarked. His torso was a patchwork of ripening bruises, and he ached from head to foot. When, after half an hour of soaking, he got out of the bath and surveyed himself in the mirror, his body seemed to be puffed up by the beating, the skin of his chest tender and tight. He was not a pretty sight.

"Tomorrow, you must go to the police," Carole told him later as they lay side by side. "And have this bastard Garvey arrested."

"I suppose so..." he said.

She leaned over him. His face was bland with fatigue. She kissed him lightly.

"I'd like to love you," she said. He did not look at her. "Why do you make it so difficult?"

"Do I?" he said, his eyelids drooping. She wanted to slide her hand beneath the bathrobe he was still wearing—she had never quite understood his coyness, but it charmed her—and caress him. But there was a certain insularity in the way he lay that signaled his wish to be left untouched, and she respected it.

"I'll turn out the light," she said, but he was already asleep.

•

The tide was not kind to Ezra Garvey. It picked up his body and played it back and forth awhile, picking at it like a replete diner toying with food he had no appetite for. It carried the corpse a mile downstream, and then tired of its burden. The current relegated it to the slower water near the banks, and there—abreast of Battersea—it became snagged in a mooring rope. The tide went out; Garvey did not. As the water level dropped he remained depending from the rope, his bloodless bulk revealed inch by inch as the tide left him, and the dawn came looking. By eight o'clock he had gained more than morning as an audience.

•

Jerry woke to the sound of the shower running in the adjacent bathroom. The bedroom curtains were still drawn. Only a fine dart of light found its way down to where he lay. He rolled over to bury his head in the pillow where the light couldn't disturb him, but his brain, once stirred, began to whirl. He had a difficult day ahead, in which he would have to make some account of recent events to the police. There would be questions asked and some of them might prove uncomfortable. The sooner he thought his story through, the more watertight it would be. He rolled over, and threw off the sheet.

His first thought as he looked down at himself was that he had not yet truly awakened but still had his face buried in the pillow and was merely dreaming this waking. Dreaming too the body he inhabited—with its budding breasts and its soft belly. This was not his body; his was of the other sex.

He tried to shake himself awake, but there was nowhere to wake to. He was here. This transformed anatomy was his—its slit, its smoothness, its strange weight—all *his*. In the hours since midnight he had been unknitted and remade in another image.

From next door the sound of the shower brought the Madonna back into his head. Brought the woman too, who had coaxed him into her and whispered, as he frowned and thrust, "Never . . . never . . . ," telling him, though he couldn't know it, that this coupling was his last as a man. They had conspired—woman and Madonna—to work this wonder upon him, and wasn't it the finest failure of his life that he would not even hold on to his own sex; that maleness itself, like wealth and influence, was promised, then snatched away again?

He got up off the bed, turning his hands over to admire their newfound fineness, running his palms across his breasts. He was not afraid, nor was he jubilant. He accepted this *fait accompli* as a baby accepts its condition, having no sense of what good or bad it might bring.

Perhaps there were more enchantments where this had come from. If so, he would go back to the Pools and find them for himself; follow the spiral into its hot heart, and debate mysteries with the Madonna. There were miracles in the world! Forces that could turn flesh inside out without drawing blood; that could topple the tyranny of the real and make play in its rubble.

Next door, the shower continued to run. He went to the bathroom door, which was slightly ajar, and peered in. Though the shower was on, Carole was not under it. She was sitting on the side of the bath, her hands pressed over her face. She heard him at the door. Her body shook. She did not look up.

"I saw . . . " she said. Her voice was guttural; thick with barely suppressed abhorrence. "Am I going mad?"

"No."

"Then what's happening?"

"I don't know," he replied simply. "Is it so terrible?"

"Vile," she said. "Revolting. I don't want to look at you. You hear me? *I don't want to see.*"

He didn't attempt to argue. She didn't want to know him, and that was her prerogative.

He slipped through into the bedroom, dressed in his stale and dirty clothes, and headed back to the Pools.

·

He went unnoticed; or rather, if anybody along his route noted a strangeness in their fellow pedestrian—a disparity between the clothes worn and the body that wore them—they looked the other way, unwilling to tackle such a problem at such an hour, and sober.

When he arrived at Leopold Road there were several men on the steps. They were talking, though he didn't know it, of imminent demolition. Jerry lingered in the doorway of a shop across the road from the Pools until the trio departed, and then made his way to the front door. He feared that they might have changed the lock, but they hadn't. He got in easily, and closed the door behind him.

He had not brought a flashlight, but when he plunged into

the labyrinth he trusted to his instinct, and it did not forsake him. After a few minutes of exploration in the benighted corridors he stumbled across the jacket which he had discarded the previous day; a few turns beyond he came into the chamber where the laughing girl had found him. There was a hint of daylight here, from the pool beyond. All but the last vestiges of that luminescence that had first led him here had gone.

He hurried on through the chamber, his hopes sinking. The water still brimmed in the pool, but almost all its light had flickered out. He studied the broth: there was no movement in the depths. *They had gone.* The mothers; the children. And, no doubt, the first cause. The Madonna.

He walked through to the shower room. She had indeed left. Furthermore, the chamber had been destroyed, as if in a fit of pique. The tiles had been torn from the walls; the pipes ripped from the plasterwork and melted in the Madonna's heat. Here and there he saw splashes of blood.

Turning his back on the wreckage, he returned to the pool, wondering if it had been his invasion that had frightened them from this makeshift temple. Whatever the reason, the witches had gone, and he, their creature, was left to fend for himself, deprived of their mysteries.

He wandered along the edge of the pool, despairing. The surface of the water was not quite calm: a circle of ripples had awakened in it and was growing by the heartbeat. He stared at the eddy as it gained momentum, flinging its arms out across the pool. The water level had suddenly begun to drop. The eddy was rapidly becoming a whirlpool, the water foaming about it. Some trap had been opened in the bottom of the pool, and the waters were draining away. Was this where the Madonna had fled? He rushed back to the far end of the pool and examined the tiles. Yes! She had left a trail of fluid behind her as she crept out of her shrine to the safety of the pool. And if this was where *she* had gone, would they not all have followed?

Where the waters were draining to he had no way of knowing. To the sewers maybe, and then to the river, and finally
out to sea. To death by drowning; to the extinction of magic.
Or by some secret channel down into the earth, to some sanctuary safe from inquiry where rapture was not forbidden.

The water was rapidly becoming frenzied as suction called
it away. The vortex whirled and foamed and spat. He studied
the shape it described. A spiral, of course, elegant and inev-
itable. The waters were sinking fast now; the splashing had
mounted to a roar. Very soon it would all be gone, the door
to another world sealed up and lost.

He had no choice: he leaped. The circling undertow snatched
at him immediately. He barely had time to draw breath before
he was sucked beneath the surface and dragged round and
round, down and down. He felt himself buffeted against the
floor of the pool, then somersaulted as he was pulled inexorably
closer to the exit. He opened his eyes. Even as he did so the
current dragged him to the brink, and over. The stream took
him in its custody and flung him back and forth in its fury.

There was light ahead. How far it lay, he couldn't calculate,
but what did it matter? If he drowned before he reached that
place, and ended his journey dead, so what? Death was no
more certain than the dream of masculinity he'd lived these
years. Terms of description fit only to be turned up and over
and inside out. The earth was bright, wasn't it, and probably
full of stars. He opened his mouth and shouted into the whirlpool, as the light grew and grew, an anthem in praise of
paradox.

BABEL'S CHILDREN

WHY COULD VANESSA NEVER RESIST THE ROAD THAT HAD no signpost marking it, the track that led to God alone knew where? Her enthusiasm for following her nose had got her into trouble often enough in the past. A near-fatal night spent lost in the Alps; that episode in Marrakech that had almost ended in rape; the adventure with the sword-swallower's apprentice in the wilds of Lower Manhattan. And yet despite what bitter experience should have taught her, when the choice lay between the marked route and the unmarked, she would always, without question, take the latter.

Here, for instance. This road that meandered toward the coast of Kithnos: what could it possibly offer her but an uneventful drive through the scrubland hereabouts—a chance encounter with a goat along the way—and a view from the cliffs of the blue Aegean. She could enjoy such a view from her hotel at Merikha Bay, and scarcely get out of bed to do so. But the other highways that led from this crossroads were so clearly *marked*: one to Loutra, with its ruined Venetian fort, the other to Driopis. She had visited neither village, and had heard that both were charming, but the fact that they were so clearly named seriously marred their attraction for her. This other road, however, though it might—indeed probably *did*—lead nowhere, at least led to an *unnamed* nowhere. That was no small recommendation. Thus fueled by sheer perversity, she set off along it.

The landscape to either side of the road (or, as it rapidly became, *track*) was at best undistinguished. Even the goats she had anticipated were not in evidence here, but then the sparse vegetation looked less than nourishing. The island was no paradise. Unlike Santorini, with its picturesque volcano, or

Mykonos—the Sodom of the Cyclades—with its plush beaches
and plusher hotels, Kithnos could boast nothing that might
draw the tourist. That, in short, was why she was here: as far
from the crowd as she could conspire to get. This track, no
doubt, would take her farther still.

The cry she heard from the hillocks off to her left was not
meant to be ignored. It was a cry of naked alarm, and it was
perfectly audible above the grumbling of her rented car. She
brought the ancient vehicle to a halt and turned off the engine.
The cry came again, but this time it was followed by a shot,
and a space, then a second shot. Without thinking, she opened
the car door and stepped out onto the track. The air was fragrant
with sand lilies and wild thyme—scents that the petrol stench
inside the car had effectively masked. Even as she breathed
the perfume she heard a third shot, and this time she saw a
figure—too far from where she stood to be recognizable, even
if it had been her husband—mounting the crown of one of
the hillocks, only to disappear into a trough again. Three or
four beats later, and his pursuers appeared. Another shot was
fired but, she was relieved to see, into the air rather than at
the man. They were warning him to stop rather than aiming
to kill. The details of the pursuers were as indistinct as those
of the escapee except that—an ominous touch—they were
dressed from head to foot in billowing black garb.

She hesitated at the side of the car, not certain of whether
she should get back in and drive away or go and find out what
this hide-and-seek was all about. The sound of guns was not
particularly pleasant, but could she possibly turn her back on
such a mystery? The men in black had disappeared after their
quarry, but she pinned her eyes to the spot they had left, and
started off toward it, keeping her head down as best she could.

Distances were deceptive in such unremarkable terrain; one
sandy hillock looked much like the next. She picked her way
among the squirting cucumber for fully ten minutes before
she became certain that she had missed the spot from which

pursued and pursuer had vanished—and by that time she was lost in a sea of grass-crested knolls. The cries had long since ceased, the shots too. She was left only with the sound of gulls, and the rasping debate of cicadas around her feet.

"Damn," she said. "Why do I do these things?"

She selected the largest hillock in the vicinity and trudged up its flank, her feet uncertain in the sandy soil, to see if the vantage point offered a view of the track she'd left, or even of the sea. If she could locate the cliffs, she could orient herself relative to the spot on which she'd left the car, and head off in that approximate direction, knowing that sooner or later she'd be bound to reach the track. But the hummock was too puny; all that was revealed from its summit was the extent of her isolation. In every direction, the same indistinguishable hills, raising their backs to the afternoon sun. In desperation, she licked her finger and put it up to the wind, reasoning that the breeze would most likely be off the sea, and that she might use that slender information to base her mental cartography upon. The breeze was negligible, but it was the only guide she had, and she set off in the direction she hoped the track lay.

After five increasingly breathless minutes of tramping up and down the hillocks, she scaled one of the slopes and found herself looking not upon her car but at a cluster of whitewashed buildings—dominated by a squat tower and ringed like a garrison with a high wall—which her previous perches had given her no glimpse of. It immediately occurred to her that the running man and his three overattentive admirers had originated here, and that wisdom probably counseled against approaching the place. But then without directions from somebody might she not wander around forever in this wasteland and never find her way back to the car? Besides, the buildings looked reassuringly unpretentious. There was even a hint of foliage peeping above the bright walls that suggested a sequestered garden within, where she might at least get some shade. Changing direction, she headed toward the entrance.

She arrived at the wrought-iron gates exhausted. Only when in sight of comfort would she concede the weight of her weariness to herself: the trudge across the hillocks had reduced her thighs and shins to quivering incompetence.

One of the large gates was ajar, and she stepped through. The yard beyond was paved, and mottled with doves' droppings: several of the culprits sat in a myrtle tree and cooed at her appearance. From the yard several covered walkways led off into a maze of buildings. Her perversity unchastened by adventure, she followed the one that looked least promising and it led her out of the sun and into a balmy passage, lined with plain benches, and out the other side into a smaller enclosure. Here the sun fell upon one of the walls, in a niche of which stood a statue of the Virgin Mary—her notorious child, fingers raised in blessing, perched upon her arm. And now, seeing the statue, the pieces of this mystery fell into place: the secluded location, the silence, the plainness of the yards and walkways—this was surely a religious establishment.

She had been godless since early adolescence and had seldom stepped over the threshold of a church in the intervening twenty-five years. Now, at forty-one, she was past recall, and so felt doubly a trespasser here. But then she wasn't seeking sanctuary, was she? Merely directions. She could ask them and get gone.

As she advanced across the sunlit stone she had that curious sensation of self-consciousness which she associated with being spied upon. It was a sensitivity her life with Ronald had sophisticated into a sixth sense. His ridiculous jealousies, which had, only three months earlier, ended their marriage, had led him to spying strategies that would not have shamed the agencies of Whitehall or Washington. Now she felt not one but several pairs of eyes upon her. Though she squinted up at the narrow windows that overlooked the courtyard, and seemed to see movement at one of them, nobody made any effort to call down to her, however. A mute order, perhaps, their vow of silence so profoundly observed that she would have to communicate in sign-language? Well, so be it.

Somewhere behind her, she heard running feet; several pairs, rushing toward her. And from down the walkway, the sound of the iron gates clanging closed. For some reason her heartbeat tripped over itself, and alarmed her blood. Startled, it leaped to her face. Her weakened legs began to quiver again.

She turned to face the owners of those urgent footsteps and as she did so caught sight of the stone Virgin's head moving a fraction. Its blue eyes had followed her across the yard and now were unmistakably following her back. She stood stock still; best not to run, she thought, with Our Lady at your back. It would have done no good to have taken flight anyway, because even now three nuns were appearing from out of the shadow of the cloisters, their habits billowing. Only their beards, and the gleaming automatic rifles they carried, fractured the illusion of their being Christ's brides. She might have laughed at this incongruity, but that they were pointing their weapons straight at her heart.

There was no word of explanation offered, but then in a place that harbored armed men dressed as nuns a glimpse of sweet reason was doubtless as rare as feathered frogs.

She was bundled out of the courtyard by the three holy sisters, who summarily searched her high and low, as though she had just razed the Vatican. She took this invasion without more than a cursory objection. Not for a moment did they take their rifle sights off her, and in such circumstances obedience seemed best. Search concluded, one of them invited her to re-dress, and she was escorted to a small room and locked in. A little while later, one of the nuns brought her a bottle of palatable retsina, and, to complete this catalogue of incongruities, the best deep-dish pizza she'd had this side of Chicago. Alice, lost in Wonderland, could not have thought it curiouser.

•

"There may have been an error," the man with the waxed mustache conceded after several hours of interrogation. She was relieved to discover he had no desire to pass as an Abbess, despite the garb of the garrison. His office—if such it was— was sparsely furnished, its only remarkable artifact a human skull, its bottom jaw missing, which sat on the desk and peered vacuously at her. He himself was better dressed; his bow-tie immaculately tied, his trousers holding a lethal crease. Beneath his calculated English, Vanessa thought she sniffed the hint of an accent. French? German? It was only when he produced some chocolate from his desk that she decided he was Swiss. His name, he claimed, was Mr. Klein.

"An error?" she said. "You're damn right there's been an error!"

"We've located your car. We have also checked with your hotel. So far, your story has been verified."

"I'm not a liar," she said. She was well past the point of courtesy with Mr. Klein, despite his bribes with the confectionery. By now it must be late at night, she guessed, though as she wore no watch and the bald little room, which was in the bowels of one of the buildings, had no windows, it was difficult to be certain. Time had been telescoped with only Mr. Klein, and his undernourished Number Two, to hold her wearied attention. "Well, I'm glad you're satisfied," she said. "Now will you let me get back to my hotel? I'm tired."

Klein shook his head. "No," he said. "I'm afraid that won't be possible."

Vanessa stood up quickly, and the violence of her movement overturned the chair. Within a second of the sound the door had opened and one of the bearded sisters appeared, pistol at the ready.

"It's all right, Stanislaus," Mr. Klein purred. "Mrs. Jape hasn't slit my throat."

Sister Stanislaus withdrew and closed the door behind him.

"Why?" said Vanessa, her anger distracted by the appearance of the guard.

"Why what?" Mr. Klein asked.

"The nuns."

Klein sighed heavily and put his hand on the coffeepot that had been brought a full hour earlier, to see if it was still warm. He poured himself half a cup before replying. "In my own opinion, much of this is redundant, Mrs. Jape, and you have my *personal* assurance that I will see you released as rapidly as is humanly possible. In the meanwhile I beg your indulgence. Think of it as a game." His face soured slightly. "They like games."

"Who do?"

Klein frowned. "Never mind," he said. "The less you know, the less we'll have to make you forget."

Vanessa gave the skull a beady eye. "None of this makes any sense," she said.

"Nor should it," Mr. Klein replied. He paused to sip his stale coffee. "You made a regrettable error in coming here, Mrs. Jape. And indeed, we made an error letting you in. Normally, our defenses are stricter than you found them. But you caught us off-guard . . . and the next thing we knew—"

"Look," said Vanessa. "I don't know what's going on here. I don't *want* to know. All I want is to be allowed to go back to my hotel and finish my holiday in peace." Judging by the expression on her interrogator's face, her appeal was not proving persuasive. "Is that so much to ask?" she said. "I haven't *done* anything, I haven't *seen* anything. What's the problem?"

Mr. Klein stood up.

"The problem," he repeated quietly to himself. "Now there's a question." He didn't attempt to answer, however. Merely called: "Stanislaus?"

The door opened, and the nun was there.

"Return Mrs. Jape to her room, will you?"

"I shall protest to my embassy!" Vanessa said, her resentment flaring. "I have rights!"

"Please," said Mr. Klein, looking pained. "Shouting will help none of us."

The nun took hold of Vanessa's arm. She felt the proximity of his pistol.

"Shall we go?" he asked politely.

"Do I have any choice?" she replied.

"No."

•

The trick of good farce, she had once been informed by her brother-in-law, a sometime actor, was that it be played with deadly seriousness. There should be no sly winks to the gallery, signaling the farceur's comic intention; no business that was so outrageous it would undermine the reality of the piece. By these stringent standards she was surrounded by a cast of experts: all willing—habits, wimples and spying Madonnas notwithstanding—to perform as though this ridiculous situation was in no way out of the ordinary. Try as she might, she could not call their bluff; not break their po-faces, not win a single sign of self-consciousness from them. Clearly she lacked the requisite skills for this kind of comedy. The sooner they realized this error and discharged her from the company, the happier she'd be.

She slept well, helped on her way by half the contents of a bottle of whiskey that some thoughtful person had left in her little room when she returned to it. She had seldom drunk so much in such a short period of time, and when—just about dawn—she was awakened by a light tapping on her door, her head felt swollen and her tongue like a suede glove. It took her a moment to orient herself, during which time the rapping was repeated, and the small window in the door opened from the other side. An urgent face was pressed to it: that of an old man, with a fungal beard and wild eyes.

"Mrs. Jape," he hissed. *"Mrs. Jape.* May we have words?"

She crossed to the door and looked through the window. The old man's breath was two parts stale ouzo to one of fresh air. It kept her from pressing too close to the window, though he beckoned her.

"Who are you?" Vanessa asked, not simply out of abstract curiosity, but because the features, sunburned and leathery, reminded her of somebody.

The man gave her a fluttering look. "An admirer," he said.

"Do I know you?"

He shook his head. "You're much too young," he said. "But I know *you.* I watched you come in. I wanted to warn you, but I didn't have time."

"Are you a prisoner here too?"

"In a manner of speaking. Tell me . . . did you see Floyd?"

"Who?"

"He escaped. The day before yesterday."

"Oh," Vanessa said, beginning to thread these dropped pearls together. "Floyd was the man they were chasing?"

"Yes. He slipped out, you see. They went after him—the clods—and left the gate open. The security is *shocking* these days"—he sounded genuinely outraged by the situation—"not that I'm not pleased you're here." There was some desperation in his eyes, she thought; some sorrow he fought to keep submerged. "We heard shots," he said. "They didn't get him, did they?"

"Not that I saw," Vanessa replied. "I went to look. But there was no sign—"

"Ha!" said the old man, brightening. "Maybe he did get away then."

It had already occurred to Vanessa that this conversation might be a trap; that the old man was her captors' dupe, and this was just another way to squeeze information from her.

But her instincts instructed her otherwise. He looked at her with such affection, and his face, which was that of a master clown, seemed incapable of forged feeling. For better or worse, she *trusted* him. She had little choice.

"Help me get out," she said. "I have to get out."

He looked crestfallen. "So soon?" he said. "You only just arrived."

"I'm not a *thief*. I don't like being locked up."

He nodded. "Of course you don't," he replied, silently admonishing himself for his selfishness. "I'm sorry. It's just that a beautiful woman . . ." He stopped himself, then began again, on a fresh tack. "I never had much of a way with words."

"Are you *sure* I don't know you from somewhere?" Vanessa inquired. "Your face is somehow familiar."

"Really?" he said. "That's very nice. We all think we're forgotten here, you see."

"All?"

"We were snatched away such a time ago. Many of us were only beginning our researches. That's why Floyd made a run for it. He wanted to do a few month's decent work before the end. I feel the same sometimes." His melancholy train halted, and he returned to her question. "My name is Harvey Gomm; Professor Harvey Gomm. Though these days I forget what I was professor *of*."

Gomm. It was a singular name, and it rang bells, but she could at present find no tune in the chimes.

"You *don't* remember, do you?" he said, looking straight into her eyes.

She wished she could lie, but that might alienate the man— the only voice of sanity she'd discovered here—more than the truth; which was:

"No . . . I don't exactly remember. Maybe a clue?"

But before he could offer her another piece of his mystery, he heard voices.

"Can't talk now, Mrs. Jape."

"Call me Vanessa."

"May I?" His face bloomed in the warmth of her benefi-
cence. "*Vanessa*."

"You *will* help me?" she said.

"As best I may," he replied. "But if you see me in company—"

"—We never met."

"Precisely. *Au revoir*." He closed the panel in the door, and
she heard his footsteps vanish down the corridor. When her
custodian, an amiable thug called Guillemot, arrived several
minutes later bearing a tray of tea, she was all smiles.

•

Her outburst of the previous day seemed to have borne some
fruit. That morning, after breakfast, Mr. Klein called in briefly
and told her that she would be allowed out onto the grounds
of the place (with Guillemot in attendance), so that she might
enjoy the sun. She was further supplied with a new set of
clothes—a little large for her, but a welcome relief from the
sweaty garments she had now worn for over twenty-four hours.
This last concession to her comfort was a curate's egg, however.
Pleased as she was to be wearing clean underwear, the fact
that the clothes had been supplied at all suggested that Mr.
Klein was not anticipating a prompt release.

How long would it be, she tried to calculate, before the
rather obtuse manager of her tiny hotel realized that she wasn't
coming back; and in that event, what would he do? Perhaps
he had already alerted the authorities; perhaps they would find
the abandoned car and trace her to this curious fortress. On
this last point her hopes were dashed that very morning, during
her constitutional. The car was parked in the laurel-tree enclosure beside the gate, and to judge by the copious blessings
rained upon it by the doves had been there overnight. Her
captors were not fools. She might have to wait until somebody
back in England became concerned and attempted to trace her

whereabouts, during which time she might well die of boredom.

Others in the place had found diversions to keep them from insanity's door. As she and Guillemot wandered around the grounds that morning she could distinctly hear voices—one of them Gomm's—from a nearby courtyard. They were raised in excitement.

"What's going on?"

"They're playing games," Guillemot replied.

"Can we go and watch?" she asked casually.

"No."

"I like games."

"Do you?" he said. "We'll play then, eh?"

This wasn't the response she'd wanted, but pressing the point might have aroused suspicion.

"Why not?" she said. Winning the man's trust could only be to her advantage.

"Poker?" he said.

"I've never played."

"I'll teach you," he replied. The thought clearly pleased him. In the adjacent courtyard the players now sent up a din of shouts. It sounded to be some kind of race, to judge by the mingled calls of encouragement, and the subsequent deflation as the winning post was achieved. Guillemot caught her listening.

"Frogs," he said. "They're racing frogs."

"I wondered."

Guillemot looked at her almost fondly, and said, "Better not."

Despite Guillemot's advice, once her attention focused on the sound of the games she could not drive the din from her head. It continued through the afternoon, rising and falling. Sometimes laughter would erupt; as often, there would be arguments. They were like children, Gomm and his friends, the way they fought over such an inconsequential pursuit as racing frogs. But in lieu of more nourishing diversions, could she blame them? When Gomm's face appeared at the door later that evening, almost the first thing she said was: "I heard you this morning, in one of the courtyards. And then this afternoon, too. You seemed to be having a good deal of fun."

"Oh, the games," Gomm replied. "It was a busy day. So much to be sorted out."

"Do you think you could persuade them to let me join you? I'm getting so bored in here."

"Poor Vanessa. I wish I could help. But it's practically impossible. We're so overworked at the moment, especially with Floyd's escape."

Overworked, she thought, *racing frogs?* Fearing to offend, she didn't voice the doubt. "What's going on here?" she said. "You're not criminals, are you?"

Gomm looked outraged. "*Criminals?*"

"I'm sorry..."

"No. I understand why you asked. I suppose it must strike you as odd... our being locked up here. But no, we're not criminals."

"What then? What's the big secret?"

Gomm took a deep breath before replying. "If I tell you," he said, "will you help us to get out of here?"

"How?"

"Your car. It's at the front."

"Yes, I saw it."

"If we could get to it, would you drive us?"

"How many of you?"

"Four. There's me, there's Ireniya, there's Mottershead, and Goldberg. Of course Floyd's probably out there somewhere, but he'll just have to look after himself, won't he?"

"It's a small car," she warned.

"We're small people," Gomm returned. "You shrink with age, you know, like dried fruit. And we're *old*. With Floyd we had three hundred and ninety-eight years between us. All that bitter experience," he said, "and not one of us *wise*."

In the yard outside Vanessa's room shouting suddenly erupted. Gomm disappeared from the door, and reappeared again briefly to murmur: "They found him. Oh my God, they found him." Then he fled.

Vanessa crossed to the window and peered through. She could not see much of the yard below, but what she could see was full of frenzied activity, sisters hithering and thithering. At the center of this commotion she could see a small figure— the runaway Floyd, no doubt—struggling in the grip of two guards. He looked to be much the worse for his days and nights of living rough, his drooping features dirtied, his balding pate peeling from an excess of sun. Vanessa heard the voice of Mr. Klein rise above the babble, and he stepped into the scene. He approached Floyd and proceeded to berate him mercilessly. Vanessa could not catch more than one in every ten words, but the verbal assault rapidly reduced the old man to tears. She turned away from the window, silently praying that Klein would choke on his next piece of chocolate.

So far, her time here had brought a curious collection of experiences: one moment pleasant (Gomm's smile, the pizza, the sound of games played in a similar courtyard), the next (the interrogation, the bullying she'd just witnessed) unpalatable. And still she was no nearer understanding what the function of this prison was: why it only had five inmates (six, if she included herself) and all so old—shrunk by age, Gomm had said. But after Klein's humiliation of Floyd she was now certain that no secret, however pressing, would keep her from aiding Gomm in his bid for freedom.

•

The Professor did not come back that evening, which disappointed her. Perhaps Floyd's recapture had meant stricter regulations about the place, she reasoned, though that principle scarcely applied to her. She, it seemed, was practically forgotten. Though Guillemot brought her food and drink he did not stay to teach her poker as they had arranged, nor was she escorted out to take the air. Left in the stuffy room without company, her mind undisturbed by any entertainment but counting her toes, she rapidly became listless and sleepy.

Indeed, she was dozing through the middle of the afternoon when something hit the wall outside the window. She got up and was crossing to see what the sound was when an object was hurled through the window. It landed with a clunk on the floor. She went to snatch a glimpse of the sender, but he'd gone.

The tiny parcel was a key wrapped in a note. "Vanessa," it read, "Be ready. Yours, in saecula saeculorum. H.G."

Latin was not her forte; she hoped the final words were an endearment, not an instruction. She tried the key in the door of her cell. It worked. Clearly Gomm didn't intend her to use it *now*, however, but to wait for some signal. *Be ready*, he'd written. Easier said than done, of course. It was so tempting, with the door open and the passageway out to the sun clear, to forget Gomm and the others and make a break for it. But H.G. had doubtless taken some risk acquiring the key. She owed him her allegiance.

After that, there was no more dozing. Every time she heard a footstep in the cloisters, or a shout in the yard, she was up and ready. But Gomm's call didn't come. The afternoon dragged on into evening. Guillemot appeared with another pizza and a bottle of Coca-Cola for dinner, and before she knew it night had fallen and another day was gone.

Perhaps they would come by cover of darkness, she thought, but they didn't. The moon rose, its seas smirking, and there was still no sign of H.G. or this promised exodus. She began to suspect the worst: that their plan had been discovered and they were all being punished for it. If so, would not Mr. Klein sooner or later root out *her* involvement? Though her part had been minimal, what sanctions might the chocolate man take

out against her? Sometime after midnight she decided that
waiting here for the ax to fall was not her style at all, and she
would be wise to do as Floyd had done, and run for it.

She let herself out of the cell, and locked it behind her,
then hurried along the cloisters, cleaving to the shadows as
best she could. There was no sign of human presence—but
she remembered the watchful Virgin, who'd first spied on her.
Nothing was to be trusted here. By stealth and sheer good
fortune she eventually found her way out into the yard in
which Floyd had faced Mr. Klein. There she paused to work
out which way the exit lay from here. But clouds had moved
across the face of the moon, and in darkness her fitful sense
of direction deserted her completely. Trusting to the luck that
had got her thus far unarrested, she chose one of the exits from
the yard, and slipped through it, following her nose along a
covered walkway which twisted and turned before leading out
into yet another courtyard, larger than the first. A light breeze
teased the leaves of two entwined laurel-trees in the center of
the yard; night insects tuned up in the walls. Peaceable as it
was, the square offered no promising route that she could see,
and she was about to go back the way she'd come when the
moon shook off its veils and lit the yard from wall to wall.

It was empty but for the laurel trees and their shadow, but
that shadow fell across an elaborate design that had been painted
onto the pavement of the yard. She stared at it, too curious
to retreat, though she could make no sense of the thing at first;
the pattern seemed to be just that: a pattern. She stalked it
along one edge, trying to fathom its significance. Then it dawned
on her that she was viewing the entire picture upside down.
She moved to the other side of the courtyard and the design
came clear. It was a map of the world, reproduced down to
the most insignificant isle. All the great cities were marked and
the oceans and continents crisscrossed with hundreds of fine
lines that marked latitudes, longitudes and much else besides.
Though many of the symbols were idiosyncratic, it was clear

that the map was rife with political detail. Contested borders; territorial waters; exclusion zones. Many of these had been drawn and redrawn in chalk, as if in response to daily intelligence. In some regions, where events were particularly fraught, the land mass was all but obscured by scribblings.

Fascination came between her and her safety. She didn't hear the footsteps at the North Pole until their owner was stepping out of hiding and into the moonlight. She was about to make a run for it, when she recognized Gomm.

"Don't move," he murmured across the world.

She did as she was instructed. Glancing around him like a besieged rabbit until he was certain the yard was deserted, H.G. crossed to where Vanessa stood.

"What are you doing here?" he demanded of her.

"You didn't come," she accused him. "I thought you'd forgotten me."

"Things got difficult. They watch us all the time."

"I couldn't go on waiting, Harvey. This is no place to take a holiday."

"You're right, of course," he said, a picture of dejection. "It's hopeless. *Hopeless*. You should make your getaway on your own. Forget about us. They'll never let us out. The truth's too terrible."

"What truth?"

He shook his head. "Forget about it. Forget we ever met."

Vanessa took hold of his spindly arm. "I will *not*," she said. "I have to know what's happening here."

Gomm shrugged. "Perhaps you should know. Perhaps the whole world should know." He took her hand, and they retreated into the relative safety of the cloisters.

"What's the map for?" was her first question.

"This is where we play," he replied, staring at the turmoil of scrawlings on the courtyard floor. He sighed. "Of course it wasn't always games. But systems decay, you know. It's an irrefutable condition common to both matter and ideas. You start off with fine intentions and in two decades... *two de-cades*..." he repeated, as if the fact appalled him afresh, "... we're playing with frogs."

"You're not making much sense, Harvey," Vanessa said. "Are you being deliberately obtuse or is this senility?"

He prickled at the accusation, but it did the trick. Gaze still fixed on the map of the world, he delivered the next words crisply as if he'd rehearsed this confession.

"There was a day of sanity, back in 1962, in which it occurred to the potentates that they were on the verge of destroying the world. Even to potentates the idea of an earth only fit for cockroaches was not particularly beguiling. If annihilation was to be prevented, they decided, our better instincts had to prevail. The mighty gathered behind locked doors at a symposium in Geneva. There had never been such a meeting of minds. The leaders of Politburos and Parliaments, Congresses, Senates—the lords of the earth—in one colossal debate. And it was decided that in the future world affairs should be overseen by a special committee, made up of great and influential minds like my own—men and women who were not subject to the whims of political favor, who could offer some guiding principles to keep the species from mass suicide. This committee was to be made up of people in many areas of human endeavor—the best of the best—an intellectual and moral elite, whose collective wisdom would bring a new golden age. That was the theory anyway."

Vanessa listened, without voicing the hundred questions his short speech had so far brought to mind. Gomm went on.

"And for a while, it worked. It really worked. There were only thirteen of us—to keep some consensus. A Russian, a few of us Europeans, dear Yoniyoko, of course, a New Zealander, a couple of Americans... We were a high-powered bunch. Two Nobel Prize–winners, myself included—"

Now she remembered Gomm, or at least where she'd once

seen that face. They had both been much younger. She a schoolgirl, taught *his* theories by rote.

"—our brief was to encourage mutual understanding between the powers-that-be, help shape compassionate economic structures and develop the cultural identity of emergent nations. All platitudes, of course, but they sounded fine at the time. As it was, almost from the beginning our concerns were *territorial*."

"Territorial?"

Gomm made an expansive gesture, taking in the map in front of him. "Helping to divide the world up," he said. "Regulating little wars so they didn't become big wars, keeping dictatorships from getting too full of themselves. We became the world's domestics, cleaning up wherever the dirt got too thick. It was a great responsibility, but we shouldered it quite happily. It rather pleased us, at the beginning, to think that we thirteen were shaping the world, and that nobody but the highest echelons of government knew that we even existed."

This, thought Vanessa, was the Napoleon syndrome writ large. Gomm was indisputably insane, but what a heroic insanity! And it was essentially harmless. Why did they have to lock him up? He surely wasn't capable of doing damage.

"It seems unfair," she said, "that you're locked away in here."

"Well, that's for our own security, of course," Gomm replied. "Imagine the chaos if some anarchist group found out where we operated from, and did away with us. We *run the world*. It wasn't meant to be that way, but as I said, systems decay. As time went by the potentates—knowing they had us to make critical decisions for them—concerned themselves more and more with the pleasures of high office and less and less with *thinking*. Within five years we were no longer advisers but surrogate overlords, juggling nations."

"What fun," Vanessa said.

"For a while, perhaps," Gomm replied. "But the glamour

faded very quickly. And after a decade or so, the pressure began
to tell. Half of the committee are already dead. Golovatenko
threw himself out of a window. Buchanan—the New Zealander—had syphilis and didn't know it. Old age caught up
with dear Yoniyoko, and Bernheimer and Sourbutts. It'll catch
up with all of us sooner or later, and Klein keeps promising
to provide people to take over when we've gone, but they don't
care. They don't give a damn! We're functionaries, that's all."
He was getting quite agitated. "As long as we provide them
with judgments, they're happy. Well"—his voice dropped to
a whisper—"we're giving it up."

Was this a moment of self-realization, Vanessa wondered.
Was the sane man in Gomm's head attempting to throw off
the fiction of world domination? If so, perhaps she could aid
the process.

"You want to get away?" she said.

Gomm nodded. "I'd like to see my home once more before
I die. I've given up so much, Vanessa, for the committee, and
it almost drove me mad." *Ah*, she thought, *he knows*. "Does
it sound selfish if I say that my life seems too great a sacrifice
to make for global peace?" She smiled at his pretensions to
power, but said nothing. "If it does, it does! I'm unrepentant.
I want out! I want—"

"Keep your voice down," she advised him.

Gomm remembered himself and nodded.

"I want a little freedom before I die. We all do. And we
thought you could help us, you see." He looked at her. "What's
wrong?" he said.

"Wrong?"

"Why are you looking at me like that?"

"You're not well, Harvey. I don't think you're dangerous,
but—"

"Wait a minute," Gomm said. "What do you think I've
been telling you? I go to all this trouble—"

"Harvey. It's a fine story."

"*Story?* What do you mean, *story?*" he said, petulantly. "Oh ... I see. You don't believe me, do you? That's it! I just told you the greatest secret in the world, and you don't believe me!"

"I'm not saying you're lying—"

"Is that it? You think I'm a lunatic!" Gomm exploded. His voice echoed around the rectangular world. Almost immediately there were voices from several of the buildings, and fast upon those the thunder of feet.

"Now look what you've done," Gomm said.

"*I've* done?"

"We're in trouble."

"Look, H.G., this doesn't mean—"

"Too late for retractions. You stay where you are—I'm going to make a run for it. Distract them."

He was about to depart when he turned back to her, caught hold of her hand, and put it to his lips.

"If I'm mad," he said, "you made me that way."

Then he was off, his short legs carrying him at a fair speed across the yard. He did not even reach the laurel trees however, before the guards arrived. They shouted for him to stop. When he failed to do so one of the men fired. Bullets ploughed the ocean around Gomm's feet.

"All right," he yelled, coming to a halt and putting his hands in the air. "*Mea culpa!*"

The firing stopped. The guards parted as their commander stepped through.

"Oh, it's you, Sidney," H.G. said to the captain. The man visibly flinched to be so addressed in front of inferior ranks.

"What are you doing out at this time of night?" Sidney demanded.

"Star gazing," Gomm replied.

"You weren't alone," the captain said. Vanessa's heart sank. There was no route back to her room without crossing the open courtyard; and even now, with the alarm raised, Guillemot would probably be checking on her.

"That's true," said Gomm. "I wasn't alone." Had she offended the old man so much he was now going to betray her? "I saw the woman you brought in—"

"Where?"

"Climbing over the wall," he said.

"Jesus wept!" the captain said, and swung around to order his men in pursuit.

"I said to her," Gomm was prattling, "I said, you'll break your neck climbing over the wall. You'd be better waiting until they open the gate—"

Open the gate. He wasn't such a lunatic, after all. "Phillipenko," the captain said, "escort Harvey back to his dormitory."

Gomm protested. "I don't need a bedtime story, thank you."

"Go with him."

The guard crossed to H.G. and escorted him away. The captain lingered long enough to murmur, "Who's a clever boy, Sidney?" under his breath, then followed. The courtyard was empty again, but for the moonlight, and the map of the world.

Vanessa waited until every last sound had died, and then slipped out of hiding, taking the route the dispatched guards had followed. It led her, eventually, into an area she vaguely recognized from her walk with Guillemot. Encouraged, she hurried on along a passageway which let out into the yard with Our Lady of the Electric Eyes. She crept along the wall, and ducked beneath the statue's gaze and out, finally, to meet the gates. They were indeed open. As the old man had protested when they'd first met, security *was.* woefully inadequate, and she thanked God for it.

As she ran toward the gates she heard the sound of boots on the gravel, and glanced over her shoulder to see the captain, rifle in hand, stepping from behind the tree.

"Some chocolate, Mrs. Jape?" said Mr. Klein.

•

"This is a lunatic asylum," she told him when they had escorted her back to the interrogation room. "Nothing more nor less. You've no right to hold me here."

He ignored her complaints.

"You spoke to Gomm," he said, "and he to you."

"What if he did?"

"What did he tell you?"

"I said, What if he did?"

"And *I* said: *What did he tell you?*" Klein roared. She would not have guessed him capable of such apoplexy. "I want to know, Mrs. Jape."

Much against her will she found herself shaking at his outburst.

"He told me nonsense," she replied. "He's insane. I think you're *all* insane."

"*What* nonsense did he tell you?"

"It was rubbish."

"I'd like to know, Mrs. Jape," Klein said, his fury abating. "Humor me."

"He said there was some kind of committee at work here that made decisions about world politics and that he was one of them. That was it, for what it's worth."

"And?"

"And I gently told him he was out of his mind."

Mr. Klein forged a smile. "Of course, this is a complete fiction," he said.

"Of course," said Vanessa. "Jesus Christ, don't treat me like an imbecile, Mr. Klein. I'm a grown woman—"

"Mr. Gomm—"

"He said he was a professor."

"Another delusion. *Mr.* Gomm is a paranoid schizophrenic. He can be extremely dangerous, given half a chance. You were pretty lucky."

"And the others?"

"Others?"

"He's not alone. I've heard them. Are they all schizophrenics?"

Klein sighed. "They're all deranged, though their conditions vary. And in their time, unlikely as it may seem, they've all been killers." He paused to allow this information to sink in. "Some of them multiple killers. That's why they have this place to themselves, hidden away. That's why the officers are armed."

Vanessa opened her mouth to ask why they were required to masquerade as nuns, but Klein was not about to give her an opportunity.

"Believe me, it's as inconvenient for me as it is irritating for you to be here," he said.

"Then let me go."

"When my investigations are complete," he said. "In the meanwhile, your cooperation would be appreciated. If Mr. Gomm or any of the other patients tries to co-opt you into some plan or other, please report them to me *immediately*. Will you do that?"

"I suppose—"

"And *please* refrain from any further escape attempts. The next one could prove fatal."

"I wanted to ask—"

"Tomorrow, maybe," Mr. Klein said, glancing at his watch as he stood up. "For now, sleep."

•

Which, she debated with herself when that sleep refused to come, of all the routes to the truth that lay before her, was the *unlikeliest* path? She had been given several alternatives: by Gomm, by Klein, by her own common sense. All of them were temptingly improbable. All, like the path that had brought her here, unmarked as to their final destination. She had suffered the consequence of her perversity in following that track of course; here she was, weary and battered, locked up with little hope of escape. But that perversity was her nature—perhaps, as Ronald had once said, the one indisputable fact about her. If she disregarded that instinct now, despite all it had brought her to, she was lost. She lay awake, turning the available alternatives over in her head. By morning she had made up her mind.

•

She waited all day, hoping Gomm would come, but she wasn't surprised when he failed to show. It was possible that events of the previous evening had landed him in deeper trouble than even he could talk his way out of. She was not left entirely to herself however. Guillemot came and went, with food, with drink—and in the middle of the afternoon—with playing cards. She picked up the gist of five-card poker quite rapidly, and they passed a contented hour or two playing, while the air carried shouts from the courtyard where the bedlamites were racing frogs.

"Do you think you could arrange for me to have a bath, or at least a shower?" she asked him when he came for her dinner tray that evening. "It's getting so that I don't like my own company."

He actually smiled as he responded. "I'll find out for you."

"Would you?" she gushed. "That's very kind."

He returned an hour later to tell her that dispensation had been sought and granted; would she like to accompany him to the showers?

"Are you going to scrub my back?" she casually inquired.

Guillemot's eyes flickered with panic at the remark, and his ears flushed beetroot red. "Please follow me," he said. Obediently, she followed, trying to keep a mental picture of their route should she want to retrace it later without her custodian.

The facilities he brought her to were far from primitive, and she regretted, walking into the mirrored bathroom, that actually washing was not high on her list of priorities. Never mind; cleanliness was for another day.

"I'll be outside the door," Guillemot said.

"That's reassuring," she replied, offering him a look she trusted he would interpret as promising, and closed the door. Then she ran the shower as hot as it would go, until steam began to cloud the room, and went down on her hands and knees to soap the floor. When the bathroom was sufficiently veiled and the floor sufficiently slick, she called Guillemot. She might have been flattered by the speed of his response, but she was too busy stepping behind him as he fumbled in the steam, and giving him a hefty push. He slid on the floor, and stumbled against the shower, yelping as scalding water met his scalp. His automatic rifle clattered to the floor, and by the time he was righting himself she had it in her hand, and pointed at his torso, a substantial target. Though she was no sharpshooter and her hands were trembling, a blind woman couldn't have missed at such a range; she knew it, and so did Guillemot. He put his hands up.

"Don't shoot."

"If you move a muscle—"

"Please . . . don't shoot."

"Now . . . you're going to take me to Mr. Gomm and the others. Quickly and quietly."

"Why?"

"Just take me," she said, gesturing with the rifle that he should lead the way out of the bathroom. "And if you try to do anything clever, I'll shoot you in the back," she said. "I know it's not very manly, but then I'm not a man. I'm just an unpredictable woman. So treat me very carefully."

"Yes."

He did as he was told, meekly, leading her out of the building and through a series of passageways that took them—or so she guessed—toward the bell tower and the complex that clustered about it. She had always assumed this, the heart of the fortress, to be a chapel. She could not have been more wrong. The outer shell might be tiled roof and whitewashed walls, but that was merely a facade; they stepped over the threshold into a concrete maze more reminiscent of a bunker than a place of worship. It briefly occurred to her that the place had been built to withstand a nuclear attack, an impression reinforced by the fact that the corridors all led *down*. If this was an asylum, it was built to house some rare lunatics.

"What is this place?" she asked Guillemot.

"We call it the Boudoir," he said. "It's where everything happens."

There was little happening at present; most of the offices off the corridors were in darkness. In one room a computer calculated its chances of independent thought, unattended; in another a telex machine wrote love letters to itself. They descended into the bowels of the place unchallenged, until, rounding a corner, they came face to face with a woman on her hands and knees, scrubbing the linoleum. The encounter startled both parties, and Guillemot was swift to take the initiative. He knocked Vanessa sideways against the wall and ran for it. Before she had time to get him in her sights, he was gone.

She cursed herself. It would be moments only before alarm bells started to ring and guards came running. She was lost if she stayed where she was. The three exits from this hallway looked equally uncompromising, so she simply made for the nearest, leaving the cleaner to stare after her. The route she took proved to be another adventure. It led her through a series of rooms, one of which was lined with dozens of clocks, all showing different times; the next of which contained upward of fifty black telephones; the third and largest was lined on every side with television screens. They rose, one upon another, from floor to ceiling. All but one was blank. The exception was showing what she first took to be a mud-wrestling contest but was in fact a poorly reproduced pornographic film.

Sitting watching it, sprawled on a chair with a beer can balanced on his stomach, was a mustachioed nun. He stood up as she entered: caught in the act. She pointed the rifle at him.

"I'm going to shoot you dead," she told him.

"Shit."

"Where's Gomm and the others?"

"What?"

"Where are they?" she demanded. "*Quickly!*"

"Down the hall. Turn left and left again," he said. Then added, "I don't want to die."

"Then sit down and shut up," she replied.

"Thank God," he said.

"Why don't you?" she told him. As she backed out of the room he fell down on his knees, while the mud wrestlers cavorted behind him.

Left and left again. The directions were fruitful: they led her to a series of rooms. She was just about to knock on one of the doors when the alarm sounded. Throwing caution to the wind, she pushed all the doors open. Voices from within complained at being awakened and asked what the alarm was ringing for. In the third room she found Gomm. He grinned at her.

"Vanessa," he said, bounding out into the corridor. He was wearing a long vest and nothing else. "You came, eh? *You came!*"

The others were appearing from their rooms, bleary with sleep. Ireniya, Floyd, Mottershead, Goldberg. She could believe, looking at their raddled faces, that they indeed had four hundred years between them.

"Wake up, you old buggers," Gomm said. He had found a pair of trousers and was pulling them on.

"The alarm's ringing," one commented. His hair, which was bright white, was almost at his shoulders.

"They'll be here soon," Ireniya said.

"No matter," Gomm replied.

Floyd was already dressed. "I'm ready," he announced.

"But we're outnumbered," Vanessa protested. "We'll never get out alive."

"She's right," said one, squinting at her. "It's no use."

"Shut up, Goldberg," Gomm snapped. "She's got a gun, hasn't she?"

"*One*," said the white-haired individual. This must be Mottershead. "One gun against all of them."

"I'm going back to bed," Goldberg said.

"This is a chance to escape," Gomm said. "Probably the only chance we'll ever get."

"He's right," the woman said.

"And what about the games?" Goldberg reminded them.

"Forget the games," Floyd told the other. "Let them stew awhile."

"It's too late," said Vanessa. "They're coming." There were shouts from both ends of the corridor. "We're trapped."

"Good," said Gomm.

"You *are* insane," she told him plainly.

"You can still shoot us," he replied, grinning.

Floyd grunted. "I don't want to get out of here *that* much," he said.

"*Threaten* it! *Threaten* it!" Gomm said. "Tell them if they try anything you'll shoot us all!"

Ireniya smiled. She had left her teeth in her bedroom. "You're not just a pretty face," she said to Gomm.

"He's right," said Floyd, beaming now. "They wouldn't dare risk us. They'll have to let us go."

"You're out of your minds," Goldberg muttered. "There's nothing out there for us." He returned to his room and slammed the door. Even as he did so the corridor was blocked off at either end by a mass of guards. Gomm took hold of Vanessa's rifle and raised it to point at his heart.

"Be gentle," he said, and threw her a kiss.

"Put down the weapon, Mrs. Jape," said a familiar voice.

Mr. Klein had appeared among the throng of guards. "Take it from me, you are completely surrounded."

"I'll kill them all," Vanessa said, a little hesitantly. Then again, this time with more feeling: "I'm warning you. I'm desperate. I'll kill them *all* before you shoot me."

"I see," said Klein quietly. "And why should you assume that I give a damn whether you kill them or not? They're insane. I told you that: all lunatics, killers..."

"We both know that isn't true," said Vanessa, gaining confidence from the anxiety on Klein's face. "I want the front gates opened and the key in the ignition of my car. If you try anything stupid, Mr. Klein, I will systematically shoot these hostages. Now dismiss your bully-boys and do as I say."

Mr. Klein hesitated, then signaled a general withdrawal.

Gomm's eyes glittered. "Nicely done," he whispered.

"Why don't you lead the way?" Vanessa suggested. Gomm did as he was instructed, and her small party snaked their way out past the massed clocks and telephones and video screens. Every step they took Vanessa expected a bullet to find her, but Mr. Klein was clearly too concerned for the health of the ancients to risk calling her bluff. They reached the open air without incident.

The guards were in evidence outside, though attempting to stay out of sight. Vanessa kept the rifle trained on the four captives as they headed through the yards to where her car was parked. The gates had been opened.

"Gomm," she whispered. "Open the car doors."

Gomm did so. He had said that age had shrunk them all, and perhaps it was true, but there were five of them to fit into the small vehicle, and it was tightly packed. Vanessa was the last to get in. As she ducked to slide into the driving seat a shot rang out, and she felt a blow to her shoulder. She dropped the rifle.

"Bastards," said Gomm.

"Leave her," somebody piped up in the back, but Gomm

was already out of the car and bundling her into the back beside Floyd. He then slid into the driving seat himself and started the engine.

"Can you drive?" Ireniya demanded.

"Of course I can bloody drive!" he retorted, and the car jerked forward through the gates, the gears grating.

Vanessa had never been shot before, and hoped—if she survived this episode—to avoid its happening again. The wound in her shoulder was bleeding badly. Floyd did his best to stanch the wound, but Gomm's driving made any really constructive help practically impossible.

"There's a track," she managed to tell him, "off that way."

"*Which way's that way?*" Gomm yelled.

"*Right! Right!*" she yelled back.

Gomm took both hands off the wheel and looked at them. "*Which is right?*"

"*For Christ's sake—*"

Ireniya, in the seat beside him, pressed his hands back onto the wheel. The car performed a tarantella. Vanessa groaned with every bump.

"I see it!" said Gomm. "I see the track!" He revved the car up, his foot slammed down on the accelerator.

One of the back doors, which had been inadequately secured, flipped open and Vanessa almost fell out. Mottershead, reaching over Floyd, yanked her back to safety, but before they could close the door it met the boulder that marked the convergence of the two tracks. The car bucked as the door was torn off its hinges.

"We needed more air in here," said Gomm, and drove on.

Theirs was not the only engine disturbing the Aegean night. There were lights behind them, and the sound of hectic pursuit. With Guillemot's rifle left in the convent, they had no sudden death to bargain with, and Klein knew it.

"Step on it!" Floyd said, grinning from ear to ear. "They're coming after us."

"I'm going as fast as I can," Gomm insisted.

"Turn off the lights," Ireniya suggested. "It'll make us less of a target."

"Then I won't be able to see the track," Gomm complained over the roar of the engine.

"So what? You're not driving on it anyhow."

Mottershead laughed, and so—against her better instincts— did Vanessa. Maybe the loss of blood was making her irresponsible, but she couldn't help herself. Four Methuselahs and herself in a three-door car driving around in the dark: only a madman would have taken this seriously. And *there* was the final and incontestable proof that these people weren't the lunatics Klein had marked them as, for they saw the humor in it too. Gomm had even taken to singing as he drove: snatches of Verdi, and a falsetto rendering of "Over the Rainbow."

And if—as her dizzied mind had concluded—these were creatures as sane as herself, then what of the tale that Gomm had told? Was that true too? Was it possible that Armageddon had been kept at bay by these few giggling geriatrics?

"They're gaining on us!" Floyd said. He was on his knees on the back seat, peering out of the window.

"We're not going to make it," Mottershead observed, his laughter barely abating. "We're all going to die."

"There!" Ireniya yelled. "There's another track! Try that! Try that!"

Gomm swung the wheel, and the car almost tipped over as it swung off the main track and followed this new route. With the lights extinguished it was impossible to see more than a glimmer of the road ahead, but Gomm's style was not about to be cramped by such minor considerations. He revved the car until the engine fairly screeched. Dust was flung up and through the gap where the door had been; a goat fled from the path ahead, avoiding death by seconds.

"Where are we going?" Vanessa yelled.

"Haven't a clue," Gomm returned. "Have you?"

Wherever they were heading, they were going at a fair speed. This track was flatter than the one they'd left, and Gomm was taking full advantage of the fact. Again, he'd taken to singing.

Mottershead was leaning out of the window on the far side of the car, his hair streaming, watching for their pursuers.

"We're losing them!" he howled triumphantly. "We're losing them!"

A common exhilaration seized all the travelers now, and they began to sing along with H.G. They were singing so loudly that Gomm couldn't hear Mottershead inform him that the road ahead seemed to disappear. Indeed H.G. was not aware that he had driven the car over the cliff until the vehicle took a nosedive and the sea came up to meet them.

•

"Mrs. Jape? Mrs. Jape?"

Vanessa woke unwillingly. Her head hurt, her arm hurt. There had been some terrible times recently, though it took her a while to remember the substance of them. Then the memories came back. The car pitching over the cliff; the cold sea rushing in through the open door; the frantic cries around her as the vehicle sank. She had struggled free, only half conscious, vaguely aware that Floyd was floating up beside her. She had said his name, but he had not answered. She said it again, now.

"Dead," said Mr. Klein. "They're all dead."

"Oh my God," she murmured. She was looking not at his face but at a chocolate stain on his waistcoat.

"Never mind them now," he insisted.

"Never mind?"

"There's more important business, Mrs. Jape. You must get up, and quickly."

The urgency in Klein's voice brought Vanessa to her feet. "Is it morning?" she said. There were no windows in the room they occupied. This was the Boudoir, to judge by its concrete walls.

"Yes, it's morning," Klein replied impatiently. "Now, will you come with me? I have something to show you." He opened the door and they stepped out into the grim corridor. A little way ahead it sounded as if a major argument was going on; dozens of raised voices, imprecations and pleadings.

"What's happening?"

"They're warming up for the Apocalypse," he replied, and led the way into the room where Vanessa had last seen the mud wrestlers. Now all the video screens were buzzing and each displayed a different interior. There were war rooms and presidential suites, cabinet offices and halls of congress. In every one of them, somebody was shouting.

"You've been unconscious two full days," Klein told her, as if this went some way to explaining the cacophony. Her head ached. She looked from screen to screen: from Washington to Hamburg to Sydney to Rio de Janeiro. Everywhere around the globe the mighty were waiting for news. But the oracles were dead.

"They're just performers," Klein said, gesturing at the shouting screens. "They couldn't run a three-legged race, never mind the world. They're getting hysterical, and their button fingers are starting to itch."

"What am *I* supposed to do about it?" Vanessa returned. This tower of Babel depressed her. "I'm no strategist."

"Neither were Gomm and the others. They might have been, once upon a time, but things soon fell apart."

"Systems decay," she said.

"Isn't *that* the truth. By the time I came here half the committee were already dead. And the rest had lost all interest in their duties—"

"But they still provided judgments, as H.G. said?"

"Oh yes."

"They ruled the world?"

"After a fashion," Klein replied.

"What do you mean: after a fashion?"

Klein looked at the screens. His eyes seemed to be on the verge of spilling tears.

"Didn't he explain? They played *games*, Mrs. Jape. When they became bored with sweet reason and the sound of their own voices, they gave up debate and took to flipping coins."

"No."

"And racing frogs of course. That was always a favorite."

"But the governments—" she protested, "—surely they didn't just accept..."

"You think they care?" Klein said, "As long as they're in the public eye what does it matter to them what verbiage they're spouting, or how it was arrived at?"

Her head spun. "All *chance*?" she said.

"Why not? It has a very respectable tradition. Nations have fallen on decisions divined from the entrails of sheep."

"It's preposterous."

"I agree. But I ask you, in all honesty, is it any more terrifying than leaving the power in *their* hands?" He pointed to the rows of irate faces. Democrats sweating that the morrow would find them without causes to espouse or applause to win; despots in terror that without instruction their cruelties would lose favor and be overturned. One premier seemed to have suffered a bronchial attack and was being supported by two of his aides; another clutched a revolver and was pointing it at the screen, demanding satisfaction. A third was chewing his toupee. Were these the finest fruit of the political tree, babbling, bullying, cajoling idiots, driven to apoplexy because nobody would tell them which way to jump? There wasn't a man or woman among them Vanessa would have trusted to guide her across the road.

"Better the frogs," she murmured, bitter thought that it was.

•

The light in the courtyard, after the dead illumination of
the bunker, was dazzlingly bright, but Vanessa was pleased to
be out of earshot of the stridency within. They would find a
new committee very soon, Klein had told her as they made
their way out into the open air: it would be a matter of weeks
only before equilibrium was restored. In the meanwhile, the
earth could be blown to smithereens by the desperate creatures
she had just seen. They needed *judgments*, and quickly.

"Goldberg is still alive," Klein said. "And he will go on with
the games; but it takes two to play."

"Why not you?"

"Because he hates me. Hates all of us. He says that he'll
only play with you."

Goldberg was sitting under the laurel trees, playing patience.
It was a slow business. His shortsightedness required him to
bring each card to within three inches of his nose to read it,
and by the time he had got to the end of the line he had
forgotten those cards at the beginning.

"She's agreed," said Klein. Goldberg didn't look up from
his game. "I said, '*she's agreed.*'"

"I'm blind, not deaf," Goldberg told Klein, still perusing
the cards. When he eventually looked up it was to squint at
Vanessa. "I told them it would end badly," he said softly, and
Vanessa knew that beneath this show of fatalism he felt the
loss of his companions acutely. "I said from the beginning, we
were here to stay. No use to escape." He shrugged, and returned
to the cards. "What's to escape *to?* The world's changed. I
know. We changed it."

"It wasn't so bad," Vanessa said.

"The world?"

"The way they died."

"Ah."

"We were enjoying ourselves, until the last minute."

"Gomm was such a sentimentalist," Goldberg said. "We never much liked each other."

A large frog jumped into Vanessa's path. The movement caught Goldberg's eye.

"Who is it?" he said.

"Who is it?"

The creature regarded Vanessa's foot balefully. "Just a frog," she replied.

"What does it look like?"

"It's fat," she said. "With three dots on its back."

"That's Israel," he told her. "Don't tread on him."

"Could we have some decisions by noon?" Klein butted in. "Particularly the Gulf situation, and the Mexican dispute, and—"

"Yes, yes, yes," said Goldberg. "Now go away."

"We could have another Bay of Pigs—"

"You're telling me nothing I don't know. Go! You're disturbing the nations." He peered at Vanessa. "Well, are you going to sit down or not?"

She sat.

"I'll leave you to it," Klein said, and retreated.

Goldberg had begun to make a sound in his throat—"*kek-kek-kek*"—imitating the voice of a frog. In response, there came a croaking from every corner of the courtyard. Hearing the sound, Vanessa stifled a smile. Farce, she had told herself once before, had to be played with a straight face, as though you believed every outrageous word. Only tragedy demanded laughter; and that, with the aid of the frogs, they might yet prevent.